SINS OF THE SAVIORS

BOOK 1:

ESCAPE FROM THE CULLING BOX

TJ Relk

For more information about the Sins of the Saviors series,
to contact the author, or to obtain permission requests, contact
Dystopian Dreams Press at: dystopiandreamspress@outlook.com and
https://dystopian-dreams-press-q2lrzu.mailerpage.io

The story, all names, characters, and incidents portrayed in this production are fictitious.

Book Cover by Miblart

First edition: 2025

ISBN: 979-8-9920471-1-0

Contents

"You don't have to burn books to destroy a culture.
Just get people to stop reading them."

Ray Bradbury

Prologue

Sweating and swearing, David rushed between cars in the crowded Non-Commissioned Officers Club parking lot. Vainly trying to shave seconds off the half hour he was late, David fixated on what his friends would say if he failed to secure a promised table. He panicked the way the young do about such things, blissfully unaware of far more anxiety-worthy events to come.

"So damn full!" he muttered as he bolted through the door, unconsciously tapping his thumb back and forth between his index and pointer finger. He spied Dan. Good old reliable Dan had already staked claim to one of the better tables.

"Relax, troop," Dan shouted above the low roar of multiple conversations. Dan leaned back in his chair and gestured for David to sit.

Relieved, he joined the ranking member of his small group. Dan was the old man of the group and a sort of mentor for the younger soldiers. Despite his self-described "chick magnet" convertible, he hadn't yet secured a wife or steady girlfriend.

No one loved classic rock night at the NCO Club more than Dan. He was not about to enjoy it at a bad table. It was busy for a Thursday night, which wasn't so unusual under the circumstances. All units were deploying in the morning and were restricted to base. The overpacked NCO club was the only on-base game in town for the soldiers to blow off a little steam one last time, free from officer observation.

David barely had time to thank his friend before Scotty, the group's whip-smart comic relief, arrived. His permanent shit-eating grin, boyish appearance, and disarming style belied his expert understanding of their unit's work, and most everyone else's. He brought with him a guy named Brian, or maybe it was Ryan, a recent arrival from another unit. Scotty had a reputation for befriending newbies and bringing them to their group until they found their own friends. David and the others were used to it by now. Dan had commandeered an extra chair in anticipation.

Larry and Tim arrived together, of course. They were a bit of a group unto themselves, a bromance that fed off like-minded sports and car enthusiasms. Solid friends both inside and outside of the foxhole.

Lastly, Peter arrived. Peter was closer in age to the others than Dan but was aging light years faster than any of them. He had just got married and moved off post. Transitioning between two worlds, he always arrived last, trying frantically to balance his affections for his new wife and his old band of brothers. The bags under his eyes showed how much it was taxing him.

David was the group's nucleus. He wasn't as book smart as Scotty, but wiser. He liked to mull over issues, both personal and professional. David was the person they approached with a vexing problem, whether a confusing regulation, the local language, or advice on girlfriends and family. More often than not, David had no immediate solutions for his many friends, but he had an open door, a ready ear, and no interest in gossip. Confiding in David was a low-risk proposition, so they kept coming back. They called him the bartender for his free consults, often doled out over drinks.

The group was deep into a debate over what beer to order when Peter called for their attention and announced Becky was pregnant. Hearty backslapping and applause broke out. Peter beamed and stood up, bestowing godparent rank for his firstborn on all six of them, even Scotty's quiet friend, whatever his name. It was a grounding moment that bonded the close group even closer.

As the band played and a river of beer washed over the club, conversations became less audible and coherent. Bursts of thoughts and emotions were increasingly fragmented but appreciated just the same, with knowing smiles and head nods. There was considerable pressure on everyone there to make it a night to remember. This was no exercise. It would be their last night out before deploying to a very real conflict that would forever change them, assuming they returned.

Tim and David danced on the table during a favorite song. Scotty defused a bar fight he had helped start. Unlucky-in-love Dan got a number from a girl (maybe out of deployment pity, but a victory nonetheless).

A friend from another unit approached the table, asking the group to help resolve a standoff in the parking lot. Dan stayed behind to mind the chairs. By the time they arrived, a small group led by Brent Triplet, a hothead everyone called Tripwire or Trip, had the band's singer hogtied in the open trunk of someone's car. A gaggle of Trip's group had surrounded the car to fend off the other band members. David, known as the unit "Trip Whisperer," passed through unchallenged.

"Trip, what are you up to, buddy?" David entered the gap between the two groups, with Larry and Tim tailing him. He smiled and put his hand on Trip's shoulder.

Trip's tense face relaxed. David recognized Trip was looking for a face-saving way to stand down. He was one of the few people Trip trusted. The arrogant rogue's tight circle of disciples were the kind of people who followed bullies, which Trip was. They were incapable of standing up to their charismatic leader, even when doing so was in his best interest.

A few minutes later, they resolved their dispute, pulled the singer from the trunk, and set him on his feet. They removed the crudely applied duct tape from his wrists and ankles. David relayed to the band what Trip had told him. *Stairway to Heaven* was a sacred song for Trip, a song he had bonded with his father over. Trip felt a "religious-like" obligation to compel the band to play the song as a tribute this pre-deployment night, David explained.

A sloppy drunk, Trip had stopped the singer while heading to the bathroom between sets to request the song. The singer told Trip they didn't know it and would need a 12-string guitar to play it. Focused on the last part of the statement, Trip and his mob surrounded the singer on the way back and took him to the parking lot with an unbaked plan to retrieve a 12-string guitar by any means necessary.

David convinced Trip to stand down because the singer didn't own a 12-string and to ensure the military police didn't lock him up. David explained the matter to the band, and the growing crowd, in such a way as to make Trip look like a noble drunk, driven "a little too far" by the power of song.

He whispered in Trip's ear, "Say it."

"Sorry, man. I just wanted to hear it," Trip confessed. He glared sheepishly at the ground but waved his arms wildly, as if doing so would convince people.

The singer was ashen-faced, but the affable, long-haired guitarist stepped up and leaned toward Trip. "All right then. We'll let this one go. Let's get on with it. Fucking behave, okay?"

The guitarist shook Trip's hand, and everyone followed the band back inside. The diplomats had won.

David stayed outside in the now quiet, almost deserted lot. It was late enough in the morning back home to call. He dialed his mother, Gale. David couldn't tell her about the deployment, but if he didn't get the call in today, he might not have a chance in the morning.

"Oh, David, so glad you called. I was about to give up," replied Gale from half a world away. "Where have you been? I've been calling forever."

David had been too busy preparing to pick up at work. Time was running out. He needed to leave soon to get some sleep, so the long, relaxed conversation with his mom would have to wait. He'd miss talking with his technophobic father, who would never buy a cell phone and was off running errands. They'd catch up after Command authorized a call from the staging area, David assumed.

It was a routine call with his mother, but, to David, it felt much heavier. His first combat deployment loomed. A soldier always downplays the risks. But beneath the bravado, anxiety. Beneath the anxiety, fear. A naked fear of imminent death that simmers dormant in the primitive core of us all until, triggered by self-preservation, it bursts through the calm facades of compassion, rationality, and civility. It cast a tense shadow over the club and created an environment lubricated for passionate, unscripted outbursts.

David buried the fear and strained to maintain a routine veneer to the call, asking about family, health, weather. But mothers sense things.

"Are you all right, son? You sound off."

"Fine, Mom. Just tired."

He wouldn't have discussed the deployment even if allowed to spare Gale unnecessary worry. He would tell her after it was over.

The troops knew little about the pending conflict, and most believed it would be avoided entirely. A short deployment to leverage a negotiated peace. No one wanted a war.

"Hey, bartender," Larry belted out from just behind him, as drunks do. David spun around. Tim and Peter were with him.

"Who's on the phone? Is that Eva?" Larry teased, inflecting Eva's name provocatively and strutting like a catwalk model.

David glared at Larry, whose eyes glinted.

"Oh, it's your mom, right?" Larry grinned. "Hi, David's mom!" he yelled toward the phone. The others followed with loud greetings.

"Go have fun with your friends. Call me back soon. Love you, sweetheart."

Under his breath and turning away from Larry, David reciprocated. "Love you, too." His friends parroted the same as David hung up and Larry folded over in laughter.

Peter said he was heading home, the first of the group to peel off. Back to his wife, with whom there would be long goodbyes and a sorrowful parting. He gave David a handshake and a shoulder pat that felt more like it wanted to be a hug. Peter and David were close and had been roommates. But they were also tough, young soldiers.

"See you tomorrow, Dave." Peter waved as he turned to find his Dodge Charger, a muscle car David knew he was planning to trade for a minivan when they returned from the conflict.

They were about to return to the NCO club when Eva and Teressa emerged out of the misty darkness and into the lighted lot. Eva and David had gone on one rather strange date—an afternoon drive to a nearby lake. It wasn't the typical dinner and movie in which a couple can get to know each other while eating or enjoying entertainment. This date required Eva and David to actually talk.

That was David's plan. Her looks drew him in—the raven hair, the expressive face, the slender yet voluptuous form that glided across the base. David already knew the body. He had designed the date to investigate the spirit.

It had begun well. They enjoyed a beautiful late afternoon walk along a pristine lake, capped off by watching the sunset while sitting on the tailgate. David expected a more fluid, relaxed conversation on the way back to base. But the truck didn't start. He had to ask his date to help push the truck up a small incline so he could jump-start it coasting down a hill.

By the time they got back, a good hour delayed, she said goodbye and fled to her quarters. David thought he'd blown it. But here she was, seeking him out.

Teressa, Eva's close friend from Alpha Company, asked Larry and Tim to join her back at the NCO Club. As the back door to the club slammed shut, Eva closed the six feet between her and David and smiled as she tilted her head.

"So," she said warmly, "how's the truck?"

"New starter." David rubbed the back of his neck, unsure where this was going. "Yeah, about the date, I wanted to apologize for making—"

"That's all right." She cut him off with a raised hand. "Really, it was sort of cute. I never had a date ask me to help fix his ride."

He shifted from foot to foot, unsure if she was being real or snarky.

"And I learned how to jump-start an old truck. Job training. Thank you." She slapped a hand over her mouth and looked up at him through her lashes. "Sorry, didn't mean it to come out like that." Eva was known for speaking with a sarcastic tone, even when she was being sincere.

"Look, I should have just called you an Uber or something. It's my fault. But I was wondering—"

Eva closed the remaining inches between them with a deep, unambiguous kiss. Pulling away, she said, "It was a wonderful date, David. I only had to run off to clean my leather shoes. They got caked in mud from pushing the truck."

"Ah, that's why you bolted."

She wrapped her slender arms around his head and body, drawing him close. David reciprocated after recovering from his initial shock.

They stood there exploring each other's mouth and body for a timeless moment until a couple of patrons loudly flung open the club's back door. David and Eva retreated around the corner to the club's loading dock. Their moment continued in relative privacy for another small eternity until the background soundtrack of cars leaving had dwindled to near silence.

Realizing the club was long closed and their friends had almost certainly left, David walked Eva to her car. They exchanged waves as her headlights soon disappeared into the fog's darkness, invisible beyond the cocoon of light the streetlights provided.

Returning to reality, David remembered he was without his truck and would have to walk 30 minutes up the hill to Charlie Company's barracks. He groaned, annoyed with himself for not thinking of it earlier. He could have asked Eva to drop him off. David channeled his pre-deployment anxiety to his legs, which propelled him up the hill on autopilot, freeing his mind to wander.

The lack of sleep is going to haunt me tomorrow. He shook his head in frustration.

A light rain began five minutes into his ascent, but the warm glow of an evening well spent shielded him. The possibility of Eva filled him with an intoxicating blend of infatuation and hope. David knew her well enough to be falling in love and not well enough to know her flaws. She was at the perfect confluence of known and unknown—new, mysterious, and perfect.

David was on a path to greater things, with the greatest of companions alongside him. The future appeared full of promise and adventure. He was certain of it. Equal parts blissful, arrogant, and ignorant.

Chapter 1: David

David recalled that final night with his friends at the club often,
playing the fond memory over and over in his head. If he failed
to reflect on it for more than a day or two, it would surface in his
dreams. It became a living thing that visited him if he did not visit
it. He obsessed over it and it possessed him—a symbiotic union.

Instead of fading over time, as most memories are destined, it
grew richer and stronger, burning ever deeper into his subconscious
with the endless revisiting. While he enjoyed its company, there was
a darker, practical reason for its preeminence. It was the only thing
tethering his frail sanity. Memories of the before time became his
only true, permanent companions.

In occasional moments of doubt, David wondered if he had
embellished those memories over the long years. Had he added or
subtracted characters, conversations, or ornamental details? Was
that large, bronze clock really above the bar at the club? It reminded
him of the one perched over his family's kitchen sink. Perhaps he
had imported it from that memory.

The other soldiers who rotated into his unit were not interested in the old man or his memories. There was a time when he tried to befriend them, even hoped they might take a message out of the box. But the time for foolish gestures had long since passed. There was no return deployment for him or anyone else. No one returned from the box.

As he finished yet another pack of bland rations after yet another day of routinized warfare, David stared blankly across the crowded chow hall, his thoughts drifting again to the memory of the night with his friends the day before the deployment. It was his happy place.

It divided his life. Before it, he was an individual, capable of independent thought and allowed some freedom to exercise those thoughts. After it, his choices disappeared. He became a number: 867-53-5150. The world became a smattering of dull, oppressive grey tones, but his pre-war memories remained in color, made all the brighter by the contrast with the present world.

He was transported to the back of the bar. His comrades were laughing, reminiscing, and drinking themselves to oblivion, cementing bonds as only those sharing mortal peril can do. Frantic merrymaking and bravado fueled by repressed fears of a conflict they knew precious little about and from which they might not return. Capping off the evening, that hauntingly beautiful woman, Ella. *Or was it Eva?* No matter, he smiled every time he saw her in his mind's eye.

The best friends he'd ever had, having the best time they would ever have. The night and the friends long gone, confirmed dead or assumed dead. All ghosts but for David and his memories.

Chapter 2: Gale

"It's time to go!" her daughter yelled through Gale's screen door, an almost invisible laser mesh. "I'll wait for you in the hover."

Mary was normally soft-spoken but had to amp up her voice to be sure her mother would hear. Gale was stubborn and wouldn't replace her eardrums. Her 97-year-old frame resisted getting up out of her living room chair. But rise she did.

It was the Fourth of July, one of the few dates she tracked with genuine excitement. Gale would be seated in a special section of the town's celebration, just to the side of the enormous stage. The arrangement made it difficult to see live parts of the local event, although she paid little attention to the local talent, anyway.

Except to introduce MyScreen clips, locals talked less and less every year, thanks to decreasing likes. Ratings don't lie and are not very tolerant. That's how democracy worked in the United Hemispheres.

It was hard to compete with the multidimensional MyScreen spectacles piped in and projected from the Goliath Network. Besides, viewers with ocular implants could close their eyes and have the illusion of facing the stage and, at the event's climax, being engulfed in an armada of fireworks designed to engage every sense. You never had to move; MyScreen would find you and give you the best seat in the house.

Gale was part of a dwindling minority who opted out of the implants. She didn't want people poking around in her head for what she considered frivolous upgrades in resolution and experience. Every year, Mary would ask her to reconsider.

Every year, Gale would say, "The projections are plenty good. Why come if you're just going to watch it in your head?"

She was right. People still came to say they were there, but they needn't have been. Live and virtual ceased to have meaningful distinction, with the former referred to as "non-enhanced."

Gale felt a little sorry for the mayor, who relished speaking about the town's distinctiveness and its contribution to country and war. Over the years, they cut his speech to five minutes, then cut it altogether and made him MC, then replaced him with a professional MC. Reminiscing in the stands, years later, she asked a couple sitting next to her what had happened to the mayor. "What's a mayor?" they replied.

She wondered how earlier generations could sit through the event back when every city councilperson was allowed a brief speech. Imagine. *Who's got time for all that?*

When their social media scores plummeted, so did their careers, and they were all let go a decade or so after the war began. *Good riddance. Not entertaining at all.*

As she made her way to the front door, Gale spied the temperature image projected above the door frame: 99 degrees. A split second of apprehension before Gale remembered she would be transported in a temperature-controlled hovercraft, elevated to her seat, and enjoy it from a large, temperature-controlled auditorium.

She would never forget the bad old days, having to stand outdoors in the heat while waiting for a parade of fire trucks, tractors, high school bands, and handmade floats of all sorts, even for her old bird watching club. Gale had almost stayed home during back-to-back years of 122-degree July Fourths, but she always found the strength to fulfill her patriotic duty year after year.

People still talked about the weather, even though progress had largely isolated them from its extremes. It was a major part of the news reports, so it had to be important. Everyone had to have an opinion about it, even those who had never experienced dangerous storms or heat waves. Gale pretended to care about the weather to avoid seeming uninformed.

As was her custom, she would pause on her way out the door at the family photos on the hallway wall. There, displayed in the center like the sun around which the other photos orbited, was a photo of her boy who had died in combat. She looked deep into the eyes of her photographed son and replayed her favorite memories of the child she had never known as a man. She teared up and drifted away. Her poor Davey, forever trapped in her mind as a promising young man who sacrificed himself for the country, for his family, for progress.

"Mom, do you need a hand?" Mary peeked through the open door.

"No, that's all right. I'm coming," Gale said as she walked the last feet to the door.

She had a bad back and knee, but with the anti-gravity assist, she moved effortlessly through the electronic screen door and to the hover. Out of muscle memory, she searched her pocket for house keys but remembered she hadn't locked her house since the 30s. No one did. Old habits rendered useless by progress.

As her daughter spoke the coordinates and the hover lifted off, Gale eagerly anticipated the Survivor Salute, when the parents of dead soldiers were asked to stand and be recognized. That was her moment, once a year, to be a hero. She vicariously basked in the adulation of her son's great accomplishment: dying for his country. Chest out and standing proud, she soaked in the stares and claps of people who would pass her by tomorrow without notice, live or in-network.

His death made her sad as well, of course. But David would want it this way. That's what they told her and what she herself had come to believe.

Chapter 3: David

David was about to take a sip of coffee when the first sonic wave hit, sending his cup to shatter against the brick-and-mortar wall. The wave ripped through him as if a blender had pulverized every organ and cell, but the blast wasn't enough to cause permanent injury.

As he regained his balance and the nausea subsided, his control officer (CO) assured the troops through their headsets that the burst was a practice round to get their attention and to "get out of the damn guard tower and calibrate the launchers!" After the soldiers scurried out of the battered hilltop building, the disembodied CO's voice continued in a more matter-of-fact tone.

"Battle starts at 0900 hours. Power up your defense shields and assume your positions!"

David turned to the window facing the enemy, blown out eons ago, with only the smallest shards of glass stubbornly clinging to the windowpane. The wave was channeled through the windowless hole, rocking him and sending his cup and its slow-roasted java to their doom. *Another casualty of war*, he thought.

He and the other few soldiers in the guard tower made their way down the stairs, grabbed their glowing shields left leaning against the wall by the tower door, and took their predetermined positions along the side of the long, barren hill below the tower. They dotted the desert landscape at precise intervals, warriors awaiting yet another "noble and just" daily battle.

As the war years rolled on, tactics changed. No longer did soldiers hide behind ramparts and defenses, taking potshots at the enemy from a safe distance. Cities were off limits, though David hadn't seen one in decades. They said warfare had returned to a more civilized age when armies didn't hide behind walls or the civilians they professed to fight for. The official narrative evoked a bygone era of warfare when modern-day knights faced their enemies with honor in open battle.

David would have said they were fighting "man to man," but today's army was half women and none of the new soldiers used such dated parlance. Man was person; mankind was personkind. References to "male," "female," and "woman" were likewise dropped as arcane and sexist, replaced everywhere by "person."

The changes made a certain sense, but David still slipped up on occasion. They demoted him for telling his troops to "fight like a man." He stopped using the phrase through a combination of conscious effort and changes in circumstance. There was no longer a need for it. Warfare had changed so radically that the word "fight" lost all meaning and became obsolete.

David had tried to change with the times but found the effort at odds with who he was. It was exhausting to be phony, and, eventually, he stopped trying. Although it conflicted with his sense of duty as a soldier, he just couldn't force himself to adapt to new rules of engagement that put his life at risk. The old army would have called that stupid. Today's military would deem such an assessment "unfair" to the enemy and tantamount to cowardice.

David maintained a will to survive that allowed him to continue living against the odds. Others prioritized orders, honor, and sacrifice. They died. He had long ago stopped his internal debate about whether his survival instinct was a sign of weakness or strength. It was just there. Like it was today.

The battle began promptly on time, with sonic waves crashing down like clockwork from the adjacent hilltops on the other side of the canyon. The Red Army was there. It had switched from ally to enemy more times than David could remember, but today it was the enemy. At least, that's what Command told them. The need for flags, raised in the air or sewn onto uniforms, was another vestige of war only he remembered. For all he knew, it was the Green or Yellow Army.

A massive blast struck about 200 feet to his right and downhill. The resulting crater obliterated a handful of his unit. A plume of dirt rose and crashed near his feet, throwing dust over his location placard. Troop ID numbers and instructions to "STAND HERE AND FACE ENEMY" were etched into the brick-sized placards.

No fucking way! he thought as he broke ranks and dove behind the dirt explosion crater. The makeshift barrier shielded him from a powerful second blast, followed by several weaker shockwaves from further afield.

The battle raged for another 20 minutes as the Red Army's sonic canon changed its target, frequency, and burst rate. Finally, the CO called for a ceasefire, which no one heard, of course. The sonic attack temporarily deafened some; others suffered broken eardrums. But they all understood the battle was over as the amber "ceasefire" light flickered in the troops' digital eyepieces.

The Blue Army triumphed. The living celebrated and cheered. But it felt forced and unenthusiastic. The Blue Army always won.

Small hovercrafts filled the sky above them. The men called them anti-grav helos or AGHs. The CO and his executive officer choreographers jumped out, assessing the smoldering battlefield, taking measurements, and directing medics to the wounded.

Along with the natural cover he surreptitiously used, David's sonic deflection shield spared him from direct shock waves. Beneath his uniform, he wore decommissioned, slick-skin body armor that mostly deflected the sonic ricochets that pulverized many of his comrades. He saved his ears with the old-school ear protection, which he slyly stashed in an ammo pouch after removing his helmet. Both adaptations were unauthorized.

He never picked the engagements he couldn't prepare for. Of the three on tap today, he passed on the chemical warfare engagement, his stash of antidotes long exhausted, and the nanobot engagement. It was getting harder to outsmart those nasty things, and David wasn't confident his old signal disruptors were up to the task.

Soon after the soldiers boarded the hovercraft, the CO read off the standard post-engagement speaking points about valor and sacrifice for the few who could hear it. Scripted talk of honoring the dead and so forth elicited a faint smirk across David's face. Perfunctory compassion at its best.

The deafened men around him were also blind, figuratively, to the stage show. David and his comrades may not have "bravely chosen their fate" as the CO put it, but David had, at least, chosen how he might die that day. Not the master of his destiny, but able to shape it to an increasing degree over the years as he learned the game. Fuck destiny.

Chapter 4: David

Being a relic has advantages. Advantages unperceived by most and all the more powerful for their invisibility.

Their hovercraft jockeyed with a dozen others for an open docking station. Bees returning to the hive. From the air, the 30-odd gleaming metal stations jutted like metal teeth from the mile-wide return bay, biting into the colorless desert.

The comparatively small, modern hub of the base was built behind the return bay. Behind that lay the remnants of a once-massive base that stretched beyond the horizon of the setting sun, like a giant snake shedding useless, dead skin.

The craft docked, the hexagonal mag-locked doors sputtered open, and weary soldiers piled out. Troops triggered a loud beep every time one walked through the entryway. Scanned and recorded, like groceries at a checkout line. David's old blue force tracker no longer activated the scanners. No one noticed amid the blur of overlapping beeps, as multiple soldiers walked through multiple entries.

At first, he thought the battery in his tracker had died, but technicians assured him many years ago that the old trackers were no longer supported. They advised him to get a forehead implant instead.

Back then, he was one of only two soldiers in the entire unit with the digital dog tags, affixed to old metal dog tags worn around your neck as soldiers had done since the old world wars. The other dog-tagged soldier died a few months later. One of the technicians told his colleague not to waste time upgrading David, as "the problem would fix itself" soon enough.

Upon disembarking, a CO would bark encouragement from the entry deck: good job, mission accomplished, well done. Shit like that. Some soldiers would smile and stand a little taller. Some exchanged dispassionate high-fives and compliments. Most walked on unaffected. They lacked the fire of his generation but were steadfast in their duties. Obedient in the extreme. Zombies.

They were doing the *right* thing. Not only did their commanders tell them so, but it was borne out by stellar approval ratings and individual patriot rankings, which boosted the social merit profiles of their family and friends as well. Network synergy rewarding good works.

After every mission, they were told they won, they were the best, and their sacrifice ensured freedom, prosperity, and popularity for their friends and families back home. They shared a creeping, unspoken realization that they would never return, an inevitability they grasped more fully the longer they fought in the box.

Command stopped trying to motivate soldiers with the hope of returning not long after the war started. Shortly after, they stopped talking about winning the war. Instead, they redirected aspirations to duty to the greater society, to those other people in that other world.

Their hopes of coming home so diluted, it eroded their will to survive, to fight, and to improvise. War became a dull, daily grind. Just another job on the glide path to death.

After turning their weapons into the armory and grounding their gear along the walls of the cavernous return bay, they would line up for post-battle screenings: muscle scans, ear scans, brain scans—a whole battery customized to that soldier's battle on that day. COs called it debriefing. Some troops called it a hot wash. Both terms meant something very different before this war.

Screenings were important individual contributions to the future good. Soldiers were valued for the data they fed into the war effort, downloaded whether alive or dead, "to analyze the enemy's weapons and tactics."

For the living, battle screenings were followed by repair. Damaged eardrums were replaced. Tears in the fabric of internal organs mended. Further down, in the critical bays, soldiers had missing hands, digits, and other smaller parts replicated organically in 15 to 30 minutes, an hour max. Technicians replaced whole limbs or other larger body parts too damaged for replication with bionic prosthetics. Replacements, whether organic or bionic, were called upgrades.

Hospitals, as David remembered them, no longer existed. Critical injury bays were sometimes called hospitals on account of their longer upgrade times. If a survivor needed multiple upgrades, and if there were lines, it could be two to three hours before he or she was whole again.

Veteran soldiers were revered for the number of upgrades they had. The more machine you were, the more of a man you became in the eyes of young soldiers. "Man" in the old sense of "tough" and "capable," a usage long replaced by "tested" or "hardcore."

David was a confusing exception. Although he always had a young face, he still looked like an old man because he was old. But an old man in this environment ought to have a few bionic limbs, an artificial eye, maybe an external respirator pack. To avoid standing out, he shaved his grey beard and head.

David waited for a critical mass of troops to complete their briefings and head for the giant bay doors. He blended in with the herd as security scanners inventoried them a final time for the night. A mess hall, barracks, and a few benches and basketball courts surrounded the outdoor courtyard down the stairs. Sometimes, he'd see some contractors or COs play ball or eat around their segregated courtyards, but troops preferred to spend their free time indoors, zoning out on the network. Identical courtyard complexes ran down the length of the docking complex, organized by company and battalion.

David grabbed a ration pack in the mess hall and waited outside its doors. Once the courtyard crowd had thinned some, he slipped down a narrow passage between the mess hall and a barrack. David walked past the back of the mess hall and the supply sheds behind it. He kept a lookout for mess hall contractors out of an abundance of caution, though they only appeared on rare occasions to fix the automation that had replaced them.

There was no need for fences or surveillance. Soldiers never ventured past their courtyards. Why would they?

After a couple of blocks of lit, well-maintained warehouses, he broke free into the abandoned part of the base and made a run for the condemned barracks where his friends awaited.

Chapter 5: Mary

Mary loved her mother. She knew this event was a highlight of her year. It was one of three where Gale was recognized as a mother of a fallen soldier, the others being Veteran's Day and Memorial Day.

The United Hemispheres had adopted many popular U.S. holidays but had been particularly clever about integrating the Fourth of July. It had waited to formally announce the new UHA Constitution on July 4th to preserve the spirit of Independence Day and include all American states in the Global War on Evil (GWoE).

The audio feed in the hover segued to President Wolfe's 30-year-old Fourth of July speech. "From this day forward, we Americans stand together against evil. We declare our Independence Day. Today, tomorrow, forever!"

The audio went back to music. The passage from Wolfe's speech needed no introduction or commentary. It was dusted off and blasted out at every memorial event. Citizens recited it from memory, particularly the last snippet, "Today, tomorrow, forever," which had become a regular Network slogan and screen saver.

On the way to the sprawling event center, Gale beamed a constant, contented smile. She nodded her head occasionally to release the enthusiasm overflowing within her. Mary reminded Gale how her father used to join her at memorial events.

"David would have been so proud to see you in the stands," Mary said, seizing the opportunity to boost her mother's already excellent spirits.

But proud of what? The sentiment ended, as it always did, without extrapolation. Normally, you were proud of some specific thing that led to some specific outcome. This was the more nebulous pride of national sacrifice. In David's case with his life; in Gale's case for losing her son.

The country remains the main character, the rest of us are merely bit players, Mary pondered. *As it should be.*

Mary knew her sister had a hard time with that notion of sacrifice. It made no sense to Jane. The country didn't have a draft. That would come later. David had known damn well what he was getting into, or should have. Her mom, in Jane's mind, was just being applauded for birthing another carcass for military cannon fodder. The state gave Gale no say in the matter. She was a bystander. Nothing more.

The way she saw it, if there was anything benevolent to be done amid all the lavish attention the country heaped on the parents of dead soldiers, it would have been saying, "Sorry your son died." But they weren't sorry. They were proud.

All this patriotic grandstanding and celebration seemed at best incongruent and at worst shameful to Jane. Like breaking out the noisemakers and party hats at a funeral. She reckoned people found it easier to be congratulated than to be sad. Celebration is more entertaining than grief, appropriate or not. People lost interest in grief, particularly other people's grief, but celebration had strong ratings sustainability.

Sorrow not only had a short shelf life but also led to tough questions about the source of the grief: millions of dead troops. Why had it occurred? Who was responsible? How could they have avoided it? How might they avoid it still?

Better to just pat people on the head for a job well done and let them feel good about themselves, good about the state. The two had become one, a symbiotic well being scaled by the Goliath Network.

Most celebrated the Network's subsummation of the individual as a means of keeping foolish and destructive egos in check. Those old enough, like Mary and Jane, remembered the days of division, strife, and fear. It made them cling all the harder to the modern age's "hard-fought peace, prosperity, and security." As a simple matter of social evolution, this victory of science and good over pagan beliefs, primitive impulses, and evil shaped the new patriotism.

Good patriots held the war as sacrosanct. No one talked about endless war anymore. It was just war. That it was unending was a given. It was right. It was needed. It was progress.

What person in their right mind would object to peoplekind's evolution? *Only a caveperson like Jane*, Mary thought. She hoped her sister would come around, embrace sanity. She wished Jane would go with them to the Fourth of July celebration, but she never did.

Once Mary thought she saw Jane out of the corner of her eye, but it was a stranger. That the woman bore only a passing resemblance to her sister belied how fervently Mary wanted Jane to be there, to change her mind, to be a different person. More like her.

Over the years, that longing had soured, turning into something darker. She resented Jane for leaving it to her to make their mother happy. She always tried to plan the Fourth of July week to avoid her mother seeing Jane, lest she poison her with negative, decadent thoughts, and perhaps cause her to question her feelings about Independence Day, about the state, and about David. Mary filled Gale's schedule with things so she wouldn't see Jane until a few days after the holiday. Then, they could talk about safer topics, perhaps the weather.

From the stands, Mary watched her mother rise for recognition with admiration alongside the parents of other soldiers killed in the eternal world war. She scanned the crowd for Jane. She never gave up on her sister. Put more cynically, she was determined to change her into something different; someone she had never been.

Chapter 6: David

David talked to the other soldiers, but he could only relate to them on a superficial level. "How's the food?" and "Helluva a shot you took out there." Their interests and world back home seemed less and less his interests and world as the years wore on. As much as it made him feel like the proverbial grumpy old man complaining about kids these days, he couldn't fight the feeling that the new recruits were boring, passive, and black-and-white copies of more colorful personalities from his past. He preferred those ghosts to the living.

Over time, they stopped playing ping-pong and pool with David in the recreation room. Movie nights turned into individual VR sessions. Around each other but not with each other. Even soldiers standing shoulder to shoulder preferred to message each other rather than talk.

After the day's mission was over and soldiers debriefed and disbursed, he would sneak away the few miles to the old, abandoned barracks of Delta 2-10. Blue Force Command had renamed and reassigned his original unit several times in the years after the deployment, but the last version, the one that stuck, was Delta 2-10.

The base used to be a sprawling city, a massive anthill of soldiers, helicopters, and armored vehicles swarming around each other. It was a shell of its former self now, at most staffed to a tenth of its former capacity. But for the fully lit area around the boarding docks, along with a handful of supporting barracks and buildings, the rest of the base had gone dark.

Delta 2-10 used to be far from the base's center, requiring the troops there to wake and walk much earlier and further than others. The big redesign in the late 30s moved the operational hub to the mission docks at the far end of the base, a short walk from Delta 2-10. After years of long marches to launch sites, the Delta 2-10 got a break. But even its proximity to the docks didn't save it, and Command shuttered it years ago.

That didn't stop David from living there. It was still hooked up to the water and electrical grid. Just close enough that he didn't have to entertain moving to the new barracks or squatting elsewhere.

Bunking there allowed him to fully unwind, detached from the automated routine and propaganda imposed on the younger troops. A place for him to resolidify his evaporating psyche and fractured sense of self. A home of sorts.

David found his bunk near the closest entryway to the giant, hanger-like complex of over 500 bunks. Along the way, he said hello to his dead friends, calling some out by name, and giving others a wave or head nod. This ritual reminded him of who he was and to honor their memory. A memorial of the mind. On a more basic level, it gave him comfort. He was, at least for a few hours a day, among friends.

He wasn't insane. At least, he didn't think so. He knew they were dead. But he also did not rule out their spirits clinging on to this world in a real way, through him. A way only visible to David. Using him to convey some message or unfinished business. Using him as much as he used them.

After grounding his gear, he wandered around while preparing to settle in for the night. He talked to Peter for a while, who was asking advice on what to write to his wife. In the war's first couple of years, Command permitted, even encouraged, correspondence with the home front. While brushing his teeth, he listened to Scotty and Tom, the unit's leading armchair philosophers, argue through the bathroom stall about their favorite subject: Does God have a side in this war? David grinned at the thought.

Before hitting the bunk for the night, he played a game of chess with Dan, the closest thing he had to a father figure in the unit. The man was notorious for talking people into playing a game he was as fervent about as he was oddly untalented. They talked about shared interests in hiking and plotted post-war excursions to the mountains. He was going to teach Dan, a Southerner, how to ski.

David noticed the sun was going down. It was time to say goodnight to the ghosts and turn off the lights. He was quite certain no one would notice a small dot of light in the otherwise vast darkness of the off-limits zone. Still, he didn't want to take the risk. He set the alarm, lay down, and wandered from waking memories of his long-dead unit to the subconscious dreams of his youth.

Had decades of resurrecting the forgotten years of a relic soldier driven David to insanity or saved him from it? He knew not and cared little. It kept him alive.

Chapter 7: Mary

"Why would you ask me to do such a thing?" Jane retorted, stepping inches from Mary's face outside her front door. "How do you think it's your job to screen who can see Mom?"

Mary was all about conflict avoidance. She preferred to have such conversations at a distance, safe in her own home, or not at all. But Mary was tired of kicking the can of this recurring conflict further down the road, so she had driven all the way to Jane's house to put the matter to rest.

After years of trying to talk around the core concern or avoid it altogether, she expected Jane's pushback. *Probably thinks I'm going to buckle after a round of her fiery indignation, true to our pattern.*

Mary had asked Jane to stay away from her mother for a while. Gale would want to talk about the Fourth and David, maybe about the war in jingoistic platitudes. Her sister would respond with opinions on all counts. Jane would anger and confuse their mother, robbing Gale of her post-Fourth of July victory lap. Mary had seen it before and did not want to see it again.

"I'm not asking you to stop seeing Mom," Mary tried to explain. "Just to give her some time to enjoy the holiday."

"Why can't I talk to her?" Jane snapped. "She's not a child. She can decide who she wants to see."

"Of course, of course. I'm just asking you to let her have this time. It helps her deal with the loss."

"Well, Mary, I'm still dealing with that myself. And Mom ... I don't think it's helpful to paper over grief with patriotic bullshit." Jane had worked herself up again, climbing out of Mary's attempt to trap her righteous anger behind common concern for their mother.

"It's not about David, or the others. It's about people shining the spotlight on themselves. About wearing the flag. Bragging about how much you support the troops when you don't even care enough to understand the conflict you are throwing them into. All this pageantry is about exploiting grief, sis, not respecting it, not dealing with it."

But Mary wasn't backing down either. "That's what I'm talking about. All you do is question. Fine, do that to yourself. But no one else wants to hear it."

There was a long pause as Jane processed Mary's unexpectedly terse, personal response. Jane broke character and changed tack from reactive to reflective. "Don't you find it strange, Mary, how we just accept things? In the old wars, you got a body, you buried it. We just got ashes. And a story."

Jane paused again as she leaned over the porch railing and stared into the horizon. "I wanted to check out the story, learn about David... how he gave his life so the rest of us could live free," Jane continued, still facing away from Mary. "You know what I found? A movie called the *Battle of the Tigris*. When you look it up on Omnipedia, it's all about the movie, news clips about the movie, interviews with the actors, budgets, ratings, all that shit. Nothing about the battle itself, no other reporting. Nothing. It's like the movie was the battle."

Mary saw an opening. She never stopped trying to change Jane's mind. "But Jane, that's it. The movie is based on a true story. That means the movie is the story, the ideal version with the important parts. It's better than what happened." She believed it—why couldn't Jane?

"Listen to me, Mary! Just because a slick CGI-5D movie feels real in your head doesn't make it real. Don't you see? Fuck! Snap out of your cartoon world. Or don't. But don't tell me your bullshit is my reality!"

"Oh please, Jane. Reality again? Really?" Mary asked rhetorically. "We all get our feeds. So, we believe what we believe and that is that person's truth. You have your truth, and I have mine. One is no better than the other."

"What you are saying is there is no truth. The truth isn't debatable; it just is," Jane retorted. She paused for a split second as the thought seemed to gain speed and catch up to her mouth.

"You're confusing opinion with truth. No, worse, confusing trivial feed preferences with truth. Fuck almighty, you are three degrees of separation from even conceptualizing the idea of truth. You can't believe in something you don't understand. And now... now you're telling me I can't believe in it? Can't speak its name because it might offend someone? Fuck it all, why don't you give me a lobotomy and be done with it! You take whatever they—"

"How dare you! Fuck you!" Mary cut her sister off mid-sentence as she closed the gap between them, nearly sending Jane off her porch. Fists shaking, Mary was done listening.

"Fuck you!" Mary repeated, snapping her head back and forth with each word, like emptying rounds from a machine gun. "You sit here above it all like you're smarter. Big words. 'Conceptualizing the idea of truth.' Can you hear how full of yourself you are? How completely a selfish bitch you are?" Mary wasn't done. "It's people like you who almost drove this country off a cliff. So, no, I don't believe in the truth. Fuck the truth! People who believe in it just want to fight for it, and then people get hurt. People like Mom."

Mary suspected Jane had never heard her say the word fuck, let alone three times. The onetime debate club president was speechless, unable to process such an assault from her sweet, mild-mannered sister.

Mary filled the silence with decades of pent-up aggression. "You believe in the truth like Uncle Ken believes in the one true God." Mary bled out the last three words with stinging sarcasm. "You are both so full of shit. Worshiping jealous gods. Why jealous? Because they're insecure. Just like you. You talk about bullshit. The truth is bullshit."

Mary stepped back, becoming self-conscious about her savage diatribe. She caught her breath, slowed her pace, and lowered the shrillness of her tone. "I'm sorry, Jane. But you have been challenging me since forever. So, let me tell you for once what I believe. Truth is relative, everything is relative. That allows us to get along. If you can't handle it, that's your problem, but stay away from Mom with your cynical poison. Let her be happy or leave her the hell alone!"

Though not as eloquent as she would have liked, Mary had finally said her piece. The screed had surprised them both. Unlike Jane, who never hesitated to share half-baked thoughts, Mary seldom verbalized feelings about anything deeper than the latest Goliath series binge or new kitchen appliance experiment.

Argument was Jane's domain, and Mary awaited the counterattack. It never came. The awkward silence signaled they were both out of verbal bullets.

Mary began to walk toward her car. She paused mid-turn. "You could let yourself be happy too, Jane." She resumed and drove away. She wondered if she'd ever see Jane again.

Chapter 8: Jane

The uncharacteristically combative and self-assured Mary had shaken Jane. Beyond Jane's unease, she had lost her dead brother to the war, and now, she was losing her living sister to the new order. They had once been close. Mary had always supported her sister, even as Jane had become a social pariah.

Jane had projected confidence in their youth, but these days it was an autopilot confidence. Mary had lived in the shadow of her sister back then, but with the sun of middle age passing above them, their relationship reversed. While Mary basked in the Network's light, it had brought only clouds to Jane's world, blurring the edges of her once sharply defined shadow, threatening to erase it. As Mary reaped the social and material rewards of Network compliance, her shadow engulfed her sister.

Jane's arrogance had cost her a great deal. Inside, she questioned her commitment to outdated beliefs, like objective truth. Omninet consensus deemed that no one could know the truth. Granting yourself that godlike power to self-determine the truth was folly, self-indulgent, and dangerous.

Her sister's notion that "everyone has their feeds" had hit home. There was no feed for Jane. Nothing for the odd subversive, argumentative, or independent citizen. Why would the Network invest feeds in such downward-trending miscreants?

"Goliath celebrates choice," a slogan that seemed counterfactual to Jane. The Omninet did indeed market feeds for a wide diversity of interests and beliefs; even Uncle Ken's archaic religious feed was still supported and upgraded. Some people fixated on a particular feed. Others developed customized diets based on multiple feeds. In the end, they all did the same thing: told people what to think and how to feel, within some reasonable parameters set by moderators. It gave the illusion of free will—feeds were, after all, recommended and customized based on individual viewing histories. In this way, you "democratically" elected moderators to police your own thoughts.

But the volume of feeds belied their superficialities. To Jane, they felt increasingly homogenized, safe, and banal—because they were. Jane saw it as the illusion of choice, Goliath's self-proclaimed "supermarket of ideas." She joked that Omninet was "more like an ice cream store with a thousand flavors, but it's still just ice cream."

Uncle Ken had subscribed to a Christian denomination feed when he was just a kid. It had merged with the other Christian denominations over time. Now, it was simply "the religious feed," providing scripture, entertainment, news, and networking apps for all major faiths. The Network combined, synced, and sanitized teachings from now-forgotten religious texts (the Bible, Koran, Verdas, etc.) for the Bikordas feed.

Jane couldn't resist challenging the intellectual rigor of his "faith-based" feed, asking Ken to explain the distinction between its "United under God" slogan and the Network slogan "United under Goliath." She often pointed out contradictions in the Bikordas at Ken's family events to "rile him up a bit." Mary had chastised her for it, which seemed to her like a mean-spirited way of taking out her frustrations with Goliath on a helpless, kind believer.

But Jane didn't see Uncle Ken as a harmless old kook. He was also a feed influencer who specialized in religious nationalism and cashed in every time a gullible dolt viewed his contributions. He hosted lavish family events because of this exploitation, during which he always reminded Jane to be grateful. She cringed every time he began a meal thanking God for the food and "our many blessings and opportunities to serve Them in Goliath."

After one such prayer, during a Ramadan Sunday feast, he had asked Jane why she never said amen. Jane dodged his question with a question, asking Ken to explain why the Bikordas required constant upgrading and merging with government documents if it was the literal word of God.

"Did you write the part about 'church is state,' Uncle Ken? There's no mention of it in the original Bible."

He asked her to leave and never invited her back.

Jane rejected the network recommendations, focused her network searches to avoid gatekeeping, and eventually opted out of all her old feeds. She had relied increasingly on old-fashioned books from old-fashioned libraries. But as virtual information made physical information obsolete, she soon had to fall back on her own collection of books and recordings. The vast majority of Network citizens ridiculed those like Jane, who traded their antique information amongst themselves, as eccentric "page hoarders."

The once-sizable minority of active dissenters disappeared. Over time, most of them had come to accept the new reality or lived lonely lives divorced from the Network. The few sites and feeds that attracted people like Jane evolved or evaporated. Dissenters migrated to other feeds and changed their beliefs to something more palatable and popular.

People stopped calling Jane and others like her free thinkers decades ago. Rebelliousness stopped being a positive construct after the riots. Thereafter, once cool rebels were considered retrograde, cancerous, even evil. Gradually, they were rebranded as dissenters, deviants, or even social terrorists for questioning or criticizing the new order.

Questioning the war was a particularly ostracizing, unpatriotic sin. But, deep in her heart, Jane owed it to David to demand answers. And now, her loyalty caused her to live a lonely life, alienating everyone and ripping everything apart.

Chapter 9: David

Everyone dies. The heart stops beating. The body is buried. Simple. Dead. Except it's not.

When humans think of the living, of each other, we are not only thinking of a physical body in the here and now. The body is a conduit for the spirit, but it is not us. When that physical assemblage of water, tissue, and bone wears down and inevitably fails, our core selves, which some call spirits or souls, live on beyond physical comprehension. Life eternal.

To say you live on in the memories of others is more than an empty platitude we comfort each other with at funerals. David didn't have to believe in a spiritual afterlife to understand that if you continue to occupy the thoughts of the living, influencing their actions, you haven't passed on. Comforting. But it also means you die a second time when people forget you.

When the war began, a soldier's personal belongings were returned home with the body for the families. This changed at some point. Bodies were removed. To where, David had no idea.

Army property was recycled into inventory and personal belongings incinerated. Soldiers were assigned to incineration duty.

David had made it a point to get to his friends' lockers before others ransacked them. He took select personal items, things he thought the families would want, that reminded him of them, and stored them behind the ceiling tiles above his bunk. This went on for many years until they decommissioned and vacated the barracks.

After that, David took them down and put them back in the lockers they had once belonged in. Some items, like Dan's chess set, he set out to remind him of better times. Memorials to dear friends.

David eventually gave up any plans of returning their belongings. Apparently, the families didn't care, or someone had ignored their concerns. He realized no one was ever going to send those items back. They would serve no greater purpose than as props in his Delta 2-10 ghost barracks.

Returning from the day's mission, David found some unknown entity had invaded the barracks and emptied the lockers. The realization that he was truly alone now manifested as a crippling whole-body ache. He dropped to his knees surrounded by sterile, empty bunks, staring into space. Reconstructing old chess games with Dan would be impossible without the chessboard and pieces.

In time, he'd forget what a chessboard even looked like. He'd forget Dan. He'd forget them all. Without the scraps of personal items scattered around the barracks to conjure them back, Dan and the rest had finally departed. Without them tethering him to this place, he plotted his escape with new urgency.

After so many years, there had to be a reason the unknown murderers of David's phantom brigade suddenly cleaned out the barracks. Maybe not today, maybe not tomorrow, but they would return. His presence and all his hidden gear, stowed above ceiling panels and in crawl spaces, would be noticed. Eventually, he would return to find the body armor, transmitters, magnetrons, EMPs, gas masks, laser knives, and the rest of his secret armory gone. Or they'd raze and bury it. Or, worse still, they would raid the place with him in it.

Dismantling his refuge would take away David's combat advantage. Without it, a long-deferred death on a culling box battlefield would find him soon enough. Only escape would change that destiny. And that would be impossible without gear.

Chapter 10: David

Days passed with no signs the phantom barrack cleaners had returned. The building remained hooked up to power and water. But time was running out.

Fearing an unexpected raid of his supplies, David began to pack extra gear on war missions, particularly medical supplies and food. Since robots took over food distribution, it had become almost impossible to steal meal packs. Humans were much easier to distract. What little food he had would be impossible to restock. Only weapons were more closely monitored. No weapons made it out of the docking bay complex.

He feared someone might question his oversized pack, which dwarfed his comrades' small daypacks and added to his already odd appearance amid much younger troops in newer uniforms. But, besides some derisive stares, no one seemed to care. If the opportunity presented itself, he would finally see what was beyond the battle sets where the forever war played out—or die trying.

They had stopped distributing maps years ago, but he had kept the old ones. They were outdated and incomplete, but he pieced them together enough to give him a picture of the larger operating space.

He had always wondered what filled the spaces between the battle sites and why their access to battlefield information kept getting narrower and narrower. Providing troops with information beyond the immediate conflict zone made sense if they wanted to win. Nothing about the war made sense to him anymore.

Then, an opportunity. After days of missions that didn't lend themselves to David's escape plans, or no missions at all, Command arranged a conflict with the Green Army. This would be a multiday skirmish on the edge of their operating space. A border war in an area he knew well. He hatched a plan.

That morning, David's booted footsteps echoed through the empty, quiet barracks for the last time. He paused at the doorway and glanced over his shoulder at the place that had been his home all these years. All the ghosts had vacated, except David himself.

He flicked the lights off. The heavy metal doors slammed like a gunshot, sealing the crypt of the Delta 2-10 behind him. David continued through the narrow passages between abandoned buildings haunted by war dead. The bright morning sun angrily cast a maze of building shadows onto David's path. The base that only yesterday seemed a warm refuge to David now revealed itself to be a cold cage of body and soul.

For a multiday engagement like this, they conducted health assessments of the troops heading out. Soldiers lined up outside the troop transport boarding gates as a CivMed, short for civilian medic, performed sitting physicals while the troops boarded.

A familiar CivMed was screening David's line. Most CivMeds hightailed it out of the box after a year tour, but David reckoned this one had been there at least four years. The troops found his chit-chatty nature exceptional, as civilians rarely engaged with soldiers. Rarer still that soldiers would engage back. Even within the ranks, they preferred wired communications to physical speech. Soldiers had grown increasingly uncomfortable with verbal communication.

Control officers, once called commanding officers, never spoke to the men outside of mission business. Soldiers only saw field COs during missions, unit COs while organizing troops before and after missions, and base COs when supervising injury bays, mess halls, or facility repairs. Soldiers were not supposed to speak with COs unless addressed. Soldiers knew nothing about their COs: not where they slept, not where they ate, and certainly not their names or personal histories. That was the order of things.

Civilians, like the CivMed, weren't always so strict about OpSec, operations security, and PDA, public displays of affection. These regulations enforced non-fraternization among COs, troops, and base civilians, punishing small talk among those entities as "undermining security and discipline." Civilians weren't used to such rules or, strictly speaking, bound by them. From time to time, they slipped up and treated troops like people.

"How's it going, old man?" the CivMed greeted as David sat down and inserted his arm in the med scanner for a variety of tests and scans. It was all automated and sterile; the CivMed didn't touch his patients or even look at them. When the scanner finished, the

CivMed could tell you if you had anything from a cold to a kidney stone.

"Going all right, Doc," David said automatically, as he always did.

"I keep telling you, old man, I'm not a doctor."

"And I keep telling you I'm not old," David retorted. It was their standard exchange. It broke the monotony and gave both men pause for a grin. A welcome dent in the endless grey churn of war in the box.

"All right, old man, let's see what I can put you on medical rest for." The CivMed looked over his screen for a few seconds. "Wow, this is unusual."

"Let me guess," David said. "Everything checks out despite my hundred years?"

"Yes, troop. Once again, you've defied the rules of time and space," the CivMed replied before changing the subject.

"So, old man, what's with all the extra gear? Planning a vacation?"

"Never can be too prepared."

"You're a real boy scout, all right."

"Was one," David said. "And you win again, Doc. Be prepared was the motto. Your knowledge of ancient history remains spot on."

"Someone's got to remember who we were, right? Or else we gonna make the same mistakes over and over, eh?"

"Yeah, right," David said. "Nobody gives a shit about the past. History is guesses from the living about the lives of the dead. The parts that interest them, at least."

"The parts that sell, right; that can be pushed into movies and feeds." They exchanged a knowing grin.

The soldier behind David cleared his throat, tapping his foot on the hollow metal floor with irritation. Even the proximity of a real discussion made the troops in line irritable and uncomfortable. The CivMed glanced at him, then back to David, changing the subject.

"You've been here since it started, right?"

David nodded. The resumed tapping of the waiting soldier's foot filled a brief, awkward silence. The CivMed leaned over the desk to David's ear.

"Do yourself a favor, old man. Don't come back this time," he hissed. Clearly, the CivMed knew things he couldn't share with David, which was concerning.

The CivMed sat back in his chair, glanced at his screen, and released the arm scanner. "You're clear, soldier," he barked like an automaton for the thousandth time. The hydraulics sighed and withdrew, releasing David's arm.

Chapter 11: Mary

"I'm saving it for when David comes home."

This wasn't the first time Mary had heard her mother speak as if David was alive. There had been a lot of such episodes lately. Earlier that evening, Mary caught her trying to switch off the 3D with the phone remote. Both were outdated devices that an iCom should have replaced decades ago, but Gale shunned the new tech.

It was going to be one of those days. Those days were coming around more frequently as her mother rounded 98. No problem with the body; science had made centenarians the new normal. But Gale's mind increasingly slipped into the past.

Mary had urged a cerebral implant but sensed her mother secretly feared it. She stopped pushing. It frustrated Mary, who embraced every new upgrade herself.

"I think David outgrew it, Mom," Mary replied. "It's really made for kids." It was a white lie. Although David had bought it when he was twelve, it was a full-sized adult bow. She was trying, again, to get Gale to clean out her garage. Despite the complete lack of economic want after decades of boom, her mom was a hard-wired hoarder.

While she kept the rest of the house in order, the garage was a mess. Precariously stacked junk piles filled it from floor to ceiling with outdated technology, old clothes, non-virtual toys, the children's artwork, and much, much more. Gale even kept wooden boards she would never need ... just in case. In case of what? In case the old woman wanted to build a treehouse?

"Why not just texture scan our Rembrandts?" Mary suggested, holding her fourth-grade painting project up to the light. The replicator could make a perfect match if she wanted to recreate them later, down to the cardboard's texture, the paper's tear, and the crayon's smell. AI could enhance the art and finish incomplete drawings. Mary had made and lost that argument many times. Today was no different.

She had once recreated one of David's paintings to prove her point. She put them side by side. Somehow, Gale picked the real one.

At the end of the evening, Mary carried out two small sacks of old things for destruction. Gale had spent the last half hour of their spring cleaning putting things back from piles Mary had targeted for "donation." The bow would remain.

Mary decided it would be the last time she'd try to push her mother to clean out the garage. The mountains and valleys of forgotten things made it a little dangerous to walk among them in there, but her mother treasured the junk. Each walk through the garage brought back fond memories, like a living photo book.

Gale had collapsed into her favorite chair, a smile on her face, still basking in the memories. It made Mary smile, too. The garage and its many useless things brought Gale happiness, Mary finally realized.

It gave Gale a sense of purpose to guard her dead son's possessions. Mary would suppress her inner neat freak and let it go.

Jane needed to stay away. She'd be arguing with Gale, trying to convince her David was dead on a day she wanted him to be alive or alive on a day she was disposed to be at peace with his passing. She'd confuse and upset Gale to make sure she "got it right." Because that was the truth and Jane was a slave to the truth. She couldn't let it go. Not for herself or anyone else.

Caring more about the truth than happiness isn't selfless devotion to a greater cause, Mary reasoned; *it's utter selfishness!*

Chapter 12: David

"What's the objective?" David asked at the mission brief, causing a ripple of silence to kill scattered pre-brief chatter.

As soon as the words left his mouth, David realized he shouldn't have uttered them. Old habits die hard. He had forgotten to suppress the desire to make sense of an operation. Make sense of anything.

He tensed up in mild anxiety and unconsciously held his breath for a moment, as if bracing for a plunge into oncoming traffic. He knew what came next. The control officer would pause and stand in the center of a ring of soldiers gathered around a holo-projector to process the unexpected question. Then, a nonsensical hyperbole would ensue. And it did.

"The objective is to protect our freedoms. We fight here so our loved ones back home can be safe. They enjoy the freedom we fight for here today." Bumper sticker ideology. But it worked, enough.

"Can I get a hooah?" the CO beckoned, asking for the military version of an amen.

"Hooah!" the group intoned loudly with forced enthusiasm.

The soldiers' Pavlovian response hung in the air, begging for vindication. They weren't used to this kind of conversation. Mission background was never provided and none was asked for. In David's time, soldiers had learned an operation's objective as a standard part of a mission brief. Now, asking for it was tantamount to a small mutiny. They went into every mission blind, assured that it was an honor and duty to serve in it.

"Freedom isn't free, sir!" David retorted with a lack of passion that contrasted sharply with the CO's jingoistic call and response. Soldiers from his time would have recognized it for what it was: sarcasm. But it went over the heads of these modern-day troops. If the CO picked up on it, he didn't let on.

"Damn straight soldier!" he replied with a ferocity that made David's bland utterance all the more sardonic.

The exchange was forgotten as soon as it was spoken. Wasted time. Still, it felt good pushing back a bit. David's inside jokes resonated with an increasingly smaller group over the years until only David got them. He was alone. It was time.

Chapter 13: Gale

Gale awoke not knowing where she was. She jolted herself up in bed in a minor panic. The sun peeked through the gaps of a vaguely familiar curtain.

A split second later, Gale remembered she was in her new home. Twelve years after moving to the new house, and it still felt new. She still expected the sun to burst through her old farmhouse's open windows, greeting her like an old friend. Years of routine had hardwired Gale to wake up early, get the kids up, and do the chores. Had someone let the chickens out or rounded up the cows for milking? She couldn't oversleep her responsibilities lest any number of farm disasters ensue.

Having overcome the immediate fear of not knowing where she was, Gale moved on to her next anxiety, being lost in time. As she pushed herself willfully out of bed and walked to the kitchen, a memory flashed by her: the last New Year's celebration. Now, she remembered the year, but not the date. More importantly, she needed to know the day of the week.

With the comforting farm routine behind her, each day imposed a different schedule. Most days, she went to the senior center in the morning, but it never struck her as something she had to do. Volunteering at the hospital on Wednesdays seemed different. She would feel terrible if she missed it and let those people down. She rushed to turn on the newspaper, which hovered in the air above the kitchen table. Thankfully, it was Tuesday.

A few minutes later, while drinking coffee, the years caught up to her consciousness, and she realized she need not have worried. There was no longer anything she had to do.

She hadn't volunteered at the hospital for years. Gale had loved holding babies at the maternity ward, but every year, there had been fewer to hold. Cured genetic diseases had obsoleted the ward. Most women preferred lab birthing as a safer, easier alternative to the traditional method, which many young mothers viewed as gross and needless. Those few with sentimental attachments to the old ways had them done at home.

Medical care had advanced exponentially. Diseases had been cured, ailments easily and quickly fixed at home, and the curse of aging had nearly lifted. Hospitals closed.

She had been active in weekly neighborhood association meetings, but those had turned into a discussion group and eventually into game night for the complex. The Network-appointed complex administrator determined association event schedules.

Gale found purpose and solace in her children—her great accomplishments. David's death had become an outsized part of her identity. Being the proud mother of a war hero shaped her waking hours and, at times, her dreams.

It gave her great satisfaction to meet with other soldiers' mothers at support groups and war commemorations. But as the war became a normal, expected part of daily life, their sacrifices turned routinized and discounted. Those events were now few and far between.

Gale tried to help her daughters, especially Mary with the grandchildren, but there was little to do. Despite Mary still acting busy, her kids were adults, she worked just two days a week, and the house cleaned itself with its networked arsenal of drones and bots. She filled her life with myriad hobbies, friendships, and trips. Gale enjoyed the free time and lack of responsibilities. Most did.

Goliath provided a good life, free from want and worry. Running the farm had become increasingly burdensome after her husband passed away, and she was happy to be free of it. Most days.

But she couldn't fully enjoy her newfound freedom from responsibilities, which also meant she was devoid of purpose. She longed for someone to need her, to have tasks that needed doing.

Gale wasn't that creative or outgoing and found herself less so as her memory and mind began to fail her. She was considering something Jane had recommended, a procedure called synapsis restoration, which rejuvenated the mind's neural pathways. It had been used for some time to treat dementia and Alzheimer's. Now, people with more routine memory problems were using it.

But Gale resisted it. No matter how safe they said it was, she buckled at the notion of a machine poking around her head. Gale didn't think she needed it, at least not yet.

As was her morning routine, Gale gradually overcame her initial discombobulation as she recollected where she was, when it was, and who she was. She persuaded herself to be content with her lot, as her present reality left her little to complain about, but also with little to care about. Those things were all behind her.

Chapter 14: David

He couldn't just let it go.

"Get your packs, Delta Company. We need to take the high ground before the hovercrafts and land crawlers get here," David barked at the troops.

A few politely stood up, but they all ignored the command. In the awkward silence, as some men glanced down at their iComs, David realized he should have known better. Still, he felt a perfunctory obligation to lead and try to win. Finally, one of the female soldiers spoke.

"Nothing personal, sergeant, but we got no OpOrds for that." She tried not to sound dismissive, but she was. No soldier inhaled without an operational order or exhaled without a subsequent order. OpOrds were piped into iComs from the network.

The soldiers all sat down or wandered off, leaving David to wallow in the vapor of his impotent commands. He wondered why they bothered assigning rank anymore if no leadership role came with it. Rank was automatic now, based on time in service –a participation trophy.

He was of an age when machines were tools to facilitate the leadership of flesh and blood humans. But it seemed to David that somewhere on the road to utopia, the machines had flipped the script on humans and used them as its tools instead. Like a deathbed atheist trying to rediscover God, David hoped that somewhere in the center of the network anthill a real person pulled the strings. Someone with compassion and wisdom and, above all, free will.

But it was increasingly hard to subscribe to such a hope as the incoming troops became ever more indifferent and obedient. No one called them that. These traits were instead referred to by the opposite, more palatable term. For example, soldiers were called "brave" when they did routine tasks. Everyone "bravely" moved onto a transport or "courageously" waited in a line.

Because words had lost meaning, facts could no longer be described or understood with any accuracy. Without facts, logic fell apart. Without the ability to apply logical rigor to statements, let alone orders, anything could be said and was believed. Nothing was questioned, as facts, logic, and truth were no longer real things to people. Situational truths swam aimlessly in an ocean of situational ethics: a hellscape of relativity without a foothold of human spirit on which to moor oneself.

David wondered if this new faith in relativity had also converted the home front. He didn't think it was possible. Soldiers were disposed to accept direction and follow orders. It was their job. Surely, civilians would be different.

The decision-making process for his troops was devoid of individual reflection. During combat ops, authoritative guidance manifested itself almost exclusively from the iCom, the communicative wristband Goliath simultaneously piped into their ocular implants. When it malfunctioned or was severed from the body, soldiers froze in place.

If you saw a soldier standing motionless as fighting raged around them, they were no longer online. David used to try to assist these vulnerable comrades, yelling in vain for them to get down or return to base. They would usually just stare at him.

"Shut up!" one snapped at him, explaining curtly that she was waiting on the next OpOrd, blood pouring out of her severed arm.

They were not quite symbiotic with their mechanical implants, yet. Their faces and voices betrayed a hint of existential human fear. Fear of death, yes. But, perhaps more so, the crushing panic of losing contact with their technological hive's guidance. They would never receive that craved next order and invariably be struck down in battle. David had stopped risking his life for them long ago.

Free from the iCom band and ocular implants, referred to as "clear vision," David reckoned he was off the controllers' virtual map. He was counting on that to escape detection.

Soldiers in the initial rollout of clear vision bragged nonstop to their comrades who didn't have them. "How do you see with your regular eyes?" they would taunt, running through the array of clear vision enhancements that appeared magically in their field of vision: infrared for night vision, OpOrds, maps, weapon and targeting data, environmental scans, and unlimited magnification. After the duty day, immersive entertainment and infinite virtual realities were at their disposal. The world wasn't just at their fingertips; it was in their heads. They felt godlike.

They failed to recognize they had exchanged fake empowerment for hidden enslavement. "Clear vision" only for the puppet masters, who now saw everything the soldiers saw. Every soldier became a personal reality show for controllers to channel surf and manipulate. Gatekeepers could now direct the throng's battles, and their lives more generally, from afar. The ultimate video game. All under the banner of improved communications and effectiveness.

The iCom recorded a soldier's every action for so-called battlefield After-Action Reviews (AARs) and unit wellness checks. David assumed artificial intelligence transcribed and analyzed every utterance for keywords. Soldiers who exhibited fear or dissension were prime targets.

Many years ago, a band of COs had approached a soldier eating in the mess hall. "Are you Nathan Jacobson?"

The soldier sitting across from David nodded.

"Did you say you wondered what you were fighting for yesterday afternoon?"

The troop was escorted away in short order for "his own damn good."

Contamination controlled.

By that point, base command regarded any questioning of war operations, even seeking clarifications, as a mental health issue. Non-compliant soldiers underwent treatment "to protect themselves and others." Once accepted as a standard part of any sane soldier's state of mind, expressing fear of combat was grounds for unit separation. Controllers treated fear and doubt as contagions to be stomped out on detection.

David watched what he said around the others even more closely after that, as the iComs of others might pick up his comments. His inside voice needed to stay buried inside, lest they flag him for unpatriotic, insubordinate, or suicidal behavior. He was surrounded.

Avoiding the collective fate of the soldiers in the box meant accepting the burdens of a solitary life. Better to die alone than to live with devils. Or worse, to become one.

Untethered to an iCom, David could pick a safer position in a trench toward the rear. Peering over the embankment, he noticed the soldiers spread out over the open valley like rifle-range targets. Backlit by the morning desert sun, they appeared to be marching right into it.

Chapter 15: David

With no defense from the high ground to obstruct them, enemy drones and escorts descended at will to the field base five minutes after battle start time, as scheduled. Although nearly everything about the war had become scripted, at least the men could choose how to fight, and die, largely as they wished within their OpOrds' parameters—the rare exception of personal choice on the modern battlefield.

And fight they did. While some of the troops mounted sky sleds for an aerial intercept, David's company fortunately received a ground defense assignment, a more survivable duty. Enemy troop transports parked on the other side of the ridge came barreling down on their own sky sleds, with armored hover transports filled with troops lumbering along behind them. Conventional arms fire filled the air as sleds faced off. In seconds, Green Army sleds were upon the ground defenders. It turned into a massive street fight. Hundreds of troops fighting along a 10-mile front well beyond the horizon.

The first wave of attacking sky sleds cut down most of his comrades standing in the open. The heavily targeted trench had to be abandoned. David crouched into a firing position behind a dirt outcropping and took out a couple of sled drivers with plasma rifle fire. As the second wave approached, he bolted to the top of the outcropping and jumped skyward to his right, timing an arm tackle to a sled driver. They both fell to the ground next to each other.

The sled driver was stunned but protected from injury by the thick, platemail-like armor suit that made sled drivers look like medieval knights. David seized the advantage and immediately flipped onto the driver, stuck his pistol under the helmet at the neck, and fired. The explosive round detonated on impact. David looked into the soldier's eyes through the visor for a split second before the round liquified those eyes and everything else trapped in the enclosed headgear. The sound of ripping bone and flesh was just audible over the roar of war as the decapitated body fell limply to the ground.

The gore of war affected him little after all these years, but David experienced moments when he crumbled and hyperventilated as the numbness abated. Looking into his victim's eyes rattled him. Eyes are the gateway to the soul and David had just extinguished both.

David's victim was a woman. He'd been told that shouldn't matter, but it did. He'd keep such outdated sentimentalities to himself to avoid being flagged, and punished, as sexist.

The unexpected physical attack on the sled driver had taken her by surprise. Modern soldiers were trained to avoid physical combat, which was considered retrograde and old-school soldiering. Pulling triggers and pushing buttons had become modern, civilized warfare.

The device committed the violent act, at least a layer removed from its master.

David wasn't just lashing out in the heat of battle. His attack had a purpose. He wasn't interested in the enemy combatant; he was after her sled. He snapped back into survival mode and took cover behind the metal sled that had skidded to a stop behind them. Fortunately, it had landed with the long bottom side facing up toward the onslaught like a shield. A significant upgrade from the small dirt mound.

David used his new rampart to maximum effect, cutting down several approaching enemy ground troops. A Green trooper jumped on top of the sled and tried to catapult himself over David. Out of instinct, David rolled on his back and fired, clipping his assaulter in midair. The round hit the gap in the soldier's armor around his armpit and blew off the arm at the shoulder. The side impact made the body spin like a propeller separated from a plane, before landing a few feet away.

Moments later, David heard a buzz above him. Enemy drones had released a barrage of nanos. Like angry locusts, the nanos were upon them, targeting the body heat signatures of anyone below. In a single motion, he lunged toward the sled driver's body and threw it over his.

He felt a nano impact and attach itself to the enemy corpse's thigh, rocking the leg off of his own. David quickly repositioned the leg. From the corner of his eye under the sled driver's body, he watched the spider-like metal creature unfold itself from its attached position and scurry into a crease in the armor. David felt the woman's body vibrate as the nano burrowed into her groin. Two others impacted the upper body in quick succession and entered through the exposed arm socket. The body's still-functioning nervous system caused it to spasm at the onslaught, requiring David to maintain a death grip on it to protect himself.

The swarm passed and an eerie silence descended on the battlefield. Deeming the immediate danger over, he pushed his human shield aside and surveilled his surroundings. The few surviving soldiers were engaged in some combination of dazed wandering, frantically trying to pull the nanos off, shouting for help, and exchanging small arms fire. Complete chaos. iComs were static. With no guidance, soldiers were left to their own primitive devices.

Although scout and battle nanos were nothing new in second-wave assaults, David was used to the devices detonating or emitting deadly sonic bursts. These drones attached to flesh and dug through it, not enough to kill, only to inflict maximum pain. David was equal parts angry and curious why his leadership would employ these non-lethal versions.

Is it to test organic tissue sensors? To save money on cheaper versions? Abject cruelty?

This relative lull in the killing lasted only a few minutes before a menacing new sound roared on the horizon and the shadow of a huge aircraft passed over them. David turned. It had been at least a year or two since he'd seen such a massive airship. But never one of this design.

Four large engines faced down at them, suspending the miles-long craft above the battlefield. These weren't the almost silent magnetic repulsors that kept hovercrafts off the ground. The craft was too high up and heavy for that.

The engines' blast sent violent bursts of superheated air at the soldiers in David's vicinity. He saw soldiers positioned under the craft's nearest engine, about a half mile east, being pelted with a potentially lethal torrent of heat, dust, and debris from the exhaust.

As the soldiers stared upward, the fighting stopped. Strange humming noises joined the engine roar. Within minutes, ominous clouds gathered where a mostly clear sky had been moments earlier, blotting out the scorching desert sun. The temperature dropped; a storm was coming. The abrasive humming reached a fever pitch. Without an order to adjust their helmet noise-canceling capability, none did so. Troops doubled over in pain.

First the thunder, barely audible under the machine's noise. Then, in an instant, streaks of lightning converged in a circle at the craft's center and a hole in its center immediately redirected them out, as if channeled through an hourglass's neck down to the battlefield below. Multitudinous lightning bursts and explosions blinded David and sent him shellshocked to the ground.

The craft departed as quickly as it arrived. The overcast sky began to break up. Once he regained his senses, David pried off his sweat-soaked helmet and lifted himself on shaky arms, gut churning at the grisly screen of smoldering corpses dotting a landscape ripped apart by heavy weapons.

The nanos appeared to be a targeting device for the sinister secondary weapon. Everyone tagged by a nano had been eliminated, ally and enemy alike: 100% success rate. This battle's organizers didn't care about winning, only about death. A phrase not used since his youth burrowed its way out of a dusty corner of his mind: war crime.

War was hell. But this wasn't war. It was worse.

Chapter 16: David

The unconscious soldier lying on a field station table took shallow breaths and turned purple from lack of blood. David ripped away the sleeve with his laser knife. He was about to apply a tourniquet to stop the bleeding. The kid would lose the hand and a few inches of arm, but if David did nothing, the young troop would bleed out. Soldiers had to make such split-second, life-and-death decisions.

"Move!" shouted a medic. Before David could process the command, the medic had pushed him aside and removed the still-loose tourniquet, sneering as he threw it back at David.

"What kind of backward shit is this?!" the medic shouted.

He pulled his organic material replicator (OMR) from his belt and positioned it over the lacerated arm where shrapnel had left the limb hanging by strings of tissue. The OMR hummed to life, cauterized the wound, and initiated a DNA analysis. Seconds later, it slowly replicated the arm, building new arm tissue at about an inch every thirty seconds.

Meanwhile, the medic activated a blood replicator. The fist-sized unit hovered above them while calibrating and scanning the wounded soldier for about twenty seconds. A network of microbot-steered needles attached to long plastic tubes descended from the unit's center like an armada of flailing octopus tentacles, attaching themselves to a variety of key arteries. Within ten seconds, blood was flowing. The soldier's color and consciousness returned.

"Fucking blood replicator, so goddamned slow," the medic growled under his breath.

Others came to assist and gawk as David collected his knife and skulked away. He climbed the steps to the top of the field station overlooking the battlefield. The setting sun cast amber light that mixed with the smoke and dust of the day's fight.

Beams of light would break through and spotlight a sliver of charred earth, occasionally a smoldering vehicle, then a smoldering body. The tragic light show with its strange melancholic beauty transfixed his gaze.

He recalled the battle and tried to make sense of it. The brigade-sized engagement was of a scale and ferocity David hadn't seen in decades. A rushed and bloodier exception to a regularized battle routine. The casualty rate was at least ten times the norm, with few left alive. The battle had begun shortly after they arrived, moving the battle start time hastily up an hour, which never happened. It lasted well after five, which never happened. All the soldiers were disorganized and unprepared, which, again, never happened.

David glimpsed an upright figure through the haze of the smoldering battlefield. This man had somehow defied the odds and survived the storms of warfare and lightning around him. Caked in dirt and blood, he had risen from the ashes. The straight-backed figure silhouetted in a hazy sunset lit an ember of hope within David, like Jesus rising defiantly from the dead.

No sooner had David spotted this kindred spirit than a field control officer marched into the scene, linked iComs to download the soldier's memories, pulled out his pistol, and shot him in the head. He abruptly turned to march back, leaving the soldier's body to plummet to the ground like a puppet with its strings cut.

From the field CO's body language, David surmised the FCO was annoyed the resurrected warrior had dared to live, which required the chore of striking him down and fetching the only thing valued about this unknown soldier, his data. An object without a soul to ungrateful puppet masters.

Every time David witnessed a CO downloading a soldier's data, whether due to an irreparable wound, irreconcilable fear, or irredeemable attitude, it seemed the kiss of death. David never saw them again and assumed they were killed. Today proved his hypothesis.

Chapter 17: David

The shuttle was late, making the troops mill about anxiously. They weren't used to changes in the meticulously arranged battle schedule. In David's early soldiering, a natural "battle tempo" of allied and enemy force actions and reactions imposed the pace of war on combatants—uncontrolled, chaotic, and unrelenting.

Now, battles started and ended on time, always after sunrise and before sunset. Transports sometimes left or returned late because of mechanical issues, but seldom by more than half an hour. Only when the battle results were unexpected did delays take longer.

New weapons had been tested, yielding unanticipated results. The lightning strikes were effective, but more destructive and unpredictable than expected. The "targeting thresholds were off significantly," he heard one field CO say to another.

More deaths and, more importantly for the organizers, damage to exercise infrastructure. A lightning strike had bent and twisted a transport dock on one of the wait station's side platforms. They gave up trying to pry it loose or bend it enough for the transport to enter.

Shuttle rope ladders were extended, adding another layer to the troops' unspoken discomfort. None were trained for this. Frantic attempts to find instruction videos on their iComs failed. Frustrated soldiers cursed their iCom bands, paced, and complained about the precarious situation.

"Fuck all, it's getting dark. What do we do now?" said a soldier close to David to no one in particular.

The FCOs failed to reconcile the agitated troops with verbal climbing instructions. The troops weren't afraid of the 40-foot climb to the hovering crafts but catatonic about starting without a command. Finally, the COs typed in the OpOrd to climb. iComs instantly glowed in a comforting visual harmony across the soldiers' arms. They robotically climbed.

It was almost dark by the time David's transport was loaded. He took care to be the last to board the final transport. One of the "veteran" troops, Sergeant Oferis, helped David up over the side.

"Ready to get back to base, old-timer?" Oferis queried. He stood up to grab one of the support straps from the ceiling, which gave David space to stand next to him. Oferis, well into his fifth year, was among the oldest of David's company and as good-natured as any of the new troops. David typically responded to small talk to reward any semblance of personality among the pliant troops. This time, he resisted the urge.

The one day he couldn't have anyone witness his presence, fate had placed the chattiest troop in his company next to him. David flat-out ignored him and jockeyed for standing space at the rear of the craft. It worked. Oferis turned to talk with another troop.

"Some scary shit getting out of here so late," Oferis said. The other troop's reply was inaudible as the transport revved up and took off.

David found Oferis's fear of pending nightfall, which was really about breaking schedule, a ridiculous contrast to his disregard of the day's battle where so many faced mortal danger and followed it to their deaths.

Despite years of living with such behavior as the new normal, David held to the old normal. His comrades, friends, and family lived there. Turning his back on that world would kill the person David imagined himself to be.

But his unwavering allegiance to that "before time" and the people in it came at a high price. Years of relentless brainwashing had worn him down, and he was tired of fighting. Death, truth be told, was of growing appeal to David. After spending his whole life running from it, he increasingly considered letting it catch up to him or even running toward it.

He questioned whether those loved ones he was fighting for loved him back. Were they concerned about him after all these years? Did they exist as he remembered them? Was it all twisted in his mind, a barely recognizable echo of a reality that never was? Was he, in fact, mad? He faced the possibility that his fealty to his idealized lost world, and the people who lived there, might be misplaced.

These were troubling questions, but David reasoned if some version of his home still existed beyond the war zone they all called the box, he deserved to find it and reconcile with it. If that world only existed as a distortion in his head, it was time to put that world and those people, and David himself, to rest.

David wasn't arrogant enough to believe he'd live long enough to find those answers, but it was a better path than what awaited him on the battlefield, where his luck would run out one day. Worse than death, which would find us all soon enough, David feared living long enough to succumb to the hive mentality that infected his comrades. Better stone dead on a quest of his own design than an undead abomination of himself, wandering the box in service of unknown, ungrateful masters.

He was done with the war.

Chapter 18: David

David had been thinking over his escape for years. Since overnight deployments became a thing of the past, the battlegrounds were all quite close to the base. The route to most of them converged in a canyon valley where a river had once flowed. Now, they called it the graveyard, so named not in honor of the fallen, but for the miles of inoperable, discarded vehicles and machines that stretched along the valley floor.

It had once been a hub to distribute incoming war machines and cargo and to process damaged machines for repair, scrap, or inventory. Over the years, Command had abandoned it, save as parking for war-damaged machines. A sad menagerie of twisted metal war casualties unceremoniously half-buried by random sandstorms. A museum of the war's many decades.

One notable exception was an area with neatly arranged rows of LAV-38s, Light Attack Vehicles. They were the last of the wheeled vehicles before hovercrafts became standard. The LAVs were delivered to the box just in time to be rendered obsolete before they could be distributed. Old war machines frozen in time and, likely, still operable. Just like David.

David waited until they cleared the edge of the graveyard, where the transports slowed to turn as the valley narrowed into a rocky canyon and curved sharply. The LAVs were parked nearby, requiring not more than an hour's walk backtracking, assuming he survived the fall.

He had gone over it a couple of hundred times in his mind. But this was different. It was real. Adrenaline pumped through his veins. A twinge of mounting fear felt good. It reminded him he was more than a physical husk. Still capable of emotion.

So caught up in the moment, David almost missed his window of opportunity as the flatbed transport cleared the turn. No more time for thinking, reflecting, processing. Just out of the peripheral vision of his comrades facing forward, David stepped back off the transport's rear edge into the swirling blur of motion beneath him. Into oblivion.

Chapter 19: David

Adrenaline surged through him as he plunged through the twilight sky for a couple of frantic seconds. David was composed enough to remember to tuck and roll with the impact.

His body spun like a rag doll over the barren landscape for about 10 yards before coming to a stop inside a thicket of brush, a rare example of vegetation reintroducing itself in the culling box. As he gazed bleary-eyed skyward through the branches, he saw the now-distant glow of the hovercraft disappear between the canyon walls.

It didn't turn around. *No one saw me jump.* He lay back and exhaled in relief.

Despite the urgent situation, David shook his head at the use of hovercraft lights at full power in a conflict zone. It illuminated the craft and made it an easy target. When he arrived in the box decades ago, military protocol would not have tolerated so much as a cigarette. Command protocols would also have ruled out a roofless hovercraft careening along a canyon floor in disputed territory, where the enemy could rain weapon fire on it with impunity. But this conflict had stopped being a normal war a very long time ago.

David rolled out from the bushes and onto his back. Searing agony from his left leg flooded his senses and drowned out the pain signatures from lesser cuts and bruises. Pain from the movement confirmed the snapping noise he'd heard on impact was from his body, not his gear.

He had stacked the deck as much as he could in favor of a successful escape, jumping ship as the hovercraft slowed to a crawl to turn into the narrow part of the canyon and wind along its curved path. Still, he had jumped from a height of five stories with a heavy pack. Injury was anticipated.

"Could have been worse," he muttered through clenched teeth.

He saw his left tibia had snapped clean out of his lower leg, pulling the fabric of his uniform tight around the protruding bone. David had been shot and wounded many times. He knew how to compartmentalize pain and treat his injuries. Time to focus.

Relying on muscle memory, David began healing himself as he'd done on countless occasions in the box. He struck a button on his armband to auto-inject a concoction of pain relievers, stimulants, and blood replication nanites. The troops still called it a "Red Bull shot," long after the drink it was named for had been banned. Only David was old enough to remember junk food. He found wicked irony in the army mandating a healthy diet for all, including soldiers marked for death.

Keeping us nice and healthy before the slaughter.

With his laser-edged knife, he cut his uniform away to reveal the bone, struggling to maintain control of the weapon through a haze of pain and dull panic.

"Damn!" he hissed as he dropped the knife from shaking hands. Luckily, it didn't go far, and he could reach it. His immediate concern was blood loss, not bone damage, but the solution to both was the same. He would have to get the bone as close to its normal position as possible before employing the "doc."

The area was full of jagged rock outcroppings, which David was lucky to have avoided. He dragged himself to a massive nearby boulder, crawled backward up on it, and flung his dangling, injured lower leg into a thigh-deep crevice in the rock. Bending at the knee, David wedged his foot and lower leg inside. *Stable enough*, he reckoned. The Red Bull shot was already dulling the pain.

It's time.

First, David positioned his bum right leg so the break angled toward the sky. Then, he curled up and jerked his body sideways, using his body's weight to push the bone back into his leg. Despite the pain meds, he screamed in agony—a cry that echoed off the canyon walls like a banshee.

The bone no longer protruded, but David sensed it was still misaligned with its counterpart inside his leg. He confirmed his suspicion by threading a finger into the wound.

"Half an inch more," he groaned. "Come on!"

He propped himself up with his right arm and tried to slam the bone the rest of the way with his left fist, striking down on the leg above the break like a hammer to get the two halves as close together as possible.

Close enough for the doc. If I don't stop, I'll pass out.

David unrolled the doc and shimmied it under his shattered leg, focusing his trembling finger enough to press the activation button. Lights on the interface blinked "operational," but the doc remained silent, save for a low buzzing sound.

Why isn't it working?

David recentered the doc until the device extended its tentacle-like metal arms around his leg. It identified the wound and generated solid matter between the arms to encase it like a cast. Then it began to hum and crackle as it replicated bone, muscle, and other tissue.

The doc was a huge advancement in combat repair tech when it was released three cycles ago. Its long, technical name didn't take, so the troops just called it a "doc." Base medical staff used larger versions.

Some soldiers began using it to fix up or save wounded comrades. That distorted after-action reports about weapon lethality, leading to flawed product follow-up. Only a year after its introduction, Command decided the troops shouldn't be issued the small field versions. For the greater good of accurate metrics, soldiers were asked to throw them in a pile for destruction.

David kept his. His humanity and instinct for self-preservation remained despite relentless efforts to train it out of him.

As the pain subsided, David presumed the technology was doing its job and relaxed enough to eat a meal bar. Drinking water was extracted by an attachment on his helmet and fed into a retractable straw.

He suddenly realized how much time had passed. As the last remnants of the desert sunset faded away, the lighting elements in his headgear activated and incrementally ramped up, creating a cone of artificial illumination wherever he directed his gaze. Outside his narrow band of stove-piped vision, it was pitch black.

Alone with his thoughts, it occurred to David that his younger Blue Force comrades would have felt terrified and alone, separated from the hive.

Not my generation.

David hadn't felt so free since before the army. The escape was already worth it.

I'm probably going to die out here, but at least it'll be on my terms.

"Free of this damned war!" he roared to an audience of one.

Chapter 20: David

After about an hour, the doc beeped. It startled David out of his medicated, post-trauma trance. He wiped away sweat from his eyes to see the monitor, which flashed "Operation completed successfully."

The pain relievers were beginning to wear off. He could feel other injuries emerging: a broken ring finger, a nasty sprained ankle, and all manner of gashes and bruises from the fall. Thankfully, his leg was painless. You could read the pain from his lesser maladies on his face, but it was bearable. Most importantly, it told him where to target repairs.

He detached the doc. The leg looked fine, just a touch swollen. David folded it at the knee and pushed his foot against the boulder—not the same as standing on it, but it seemed fine. The doc had mended the bone and torn tissues.

Relieved, David turned his attention to his sprained ankle, wrapped the doc around it, and pushed "Activate." In seconds, the pain withdrew. In a few minutes, it was as good as new. An hour into

David's self-treatment, a red panel on the doc pulsed. "Device at 20 percent power. Recharge recommended."

Damn doc! Remaining flesh wounds won't slow me down, so I'll save the charge. Fixed the worst of it, but I'm screwed if I need it again for a big injury. Can't afford a gunfight.

With no iCom band or ocular implants, David should have been off-network. He supposed no one would miss him. But what if there was a tracking device in his equipment? What if they noticed he wasn't at the medical debrief? It was time to move on. David initiated the second phase of his plan.

He ripped off a dangling uniform sleeve and used strips of it to tie off a couple of wounds that might otherwise have bled when moving. When he tried walking, his back ached from a combination of impact bruises and pulling his bum leg behind him. He winced each time he had to swing it around, leaving a trail of half circles in the dusty canyon. The leg was still stiff and slightly numb below the break, typical of freshly replicated tissue. However, in another hour, it would be back to normal.

His body a tapestry of greater and lesser pains, a limping David started doubling back to the vast mechanical graveyard he had passed over in the hovercraft. For the last couple of years, his unit had regularly returned to base along this canyon route. This gave him ample time to contemplate his drop point. Not only was it at one of the lowest, slowest points of the hovercraft's journey back to base, it was also within an hour's walk of the maze.

They called it the maze because of the neat rows of parked, unused vehicles on the northern edge of the mechanical graveyard, in contrast to the more chaotic placement of older vehicles towed and dumped further south for repair or scrap. The widest part of the canyon had been the repository for both incoming and outgoing war machines for the first 16 years of the war, but, after hovercraft made wheeled vehicles obsolete, there was no longer a need for the convey routes leading to the hub. The churn of war machines to the canyon abruptly stopped and tens of thousands of battle-scarred wheeled and tracked vehicles met an inglorious retirement in the desert sun.

The veteran fugitive had outlived them all. David had burned an aerial map of the area into his mind, but at ground level and at night, it looked different. He began tapping his thumb alternatively with index and pointer finger, his signature nervous tick. The night helped to obscure his escape, but it also concealed landmarks to guide him through the maze to the Light Armored Vehicles he sought. His night vision worked, but it had been years since he had to use it.

David was beginning to wonder if he had lost his way when he glimpsed rows of LAV-38s up ahead. No new car smell or shine after so many years in the desert, but otherwise preserved and unused. They had come right off the assembly line before being shipped, parked, and forgotten.

The door of the nearest LAV swung open easily; only a creak from long-dormant hinges hinted at its age. David positioned himself in the driver's seat. He couldn't remember the last time he had driven a wheeled vehicle, but grabbing the wheel brought it all back.

David closed his eyes for a moment to let the past flow over him. He had learned to indulge memories when they came, lest he forget them forever in the suffocating isolation of the box, where there was no past and no future beyond the next mission. He remembered learning to drive in his first clunker truck, which he had bought cheap from an aging aunt who couldn't drive anymore. For this steal of a deal, David agreed to drive her to the store on weekends. He was among the first in his grade to drive. Freedom, or at least the illusion of it.

The hopeful warrior smiled and reached for the start button. Plasma batteries boasted almost limitless power and maintained their charges when unused. But a lifeless, hollow click mocked him. The LAV failed to start.

David's heart sank lower and lower each time he hit the starter. *Nothing.* He staggered out of the vehicle to peek underneath. There was a small pile of dead rats below the battery housing. He surmised the vermin had crawled into the battery compartment and attempted to eat away at its plasma hoses, killing them and the battery.

The box's few green areas had withered away in the early days of the war. The surviving animals became increasingly desperate and ate anything. Birds and varmints of all varieties converged on battlegrounds despite the noise and commotion, drawn by the smell of the soldiers' food and blood. Eventually, though, even these desperate scavengers stopped coming.

Not knowing what else to do, he punched the vehicle, which only hurt his hand. Angry with himself and his situation, David paced back and forward in the dark, his hands a blur of nervous, fidgeting digits. He'd fought to stay alive all this time, just to die like the rats under the LAV. The graveyard moniker suddenly became personal.

He walked along the edge of the LAVs until he had calmed himself enough to try a vehicle at the other end of the lot closer to the canyon wall. Its front end was mostly buried in the canyon's sandy dirt, which years of desert winds had flung to the end of the LAV column. David reckoned the rats might have had a harder time getting to its sand-encased plasma hoses. The air intake and exhaust snaked up the vehicle almost to the roof, allowing the engine to breathe. The front doors would need digging up, so he climbed in from the back hatch instead. It roared to glorious life.

His plans once again on track, David floored the accelerator forward and backward to rock the LAV free. Eventually, the LAV's massive tires overcame the sandbank, and he backed it out. He drove up to the once-paved, now dirt-covered highway leading up the canyon wall and unrolled topographical maps he had hidden away for decades on the LAV's hood. Old school soldiers like David knew how to live by compass and map, while younger soldiers had no idea what North was or why it mattered. iComs told them where to go, when to go, and what to do once they arrived. They wouldn't recognize a paper map or understand the value of charting a course themselves.

Over the years, soldiers had been given an ever-smaller segment of the battlefield to view. At this point, only the few kilometers around their daily exercise site were piped into their iComs and implants. David was the unit's sole remaining soldier with any idea of the geography of the box or where they were in it. Satisfied he was on track, he pieced together his outdated maps and drove off into the night, lights off and in a hurry to put as much real estate as possible between him and the well-traveled canyon route.

Between his helmet's drop-down night vision goggles and the half-crescent moonlight, the highway was lit up like the yellow brick road. As he crested the ridgeline in the reanimated LAV, the oppressively vast wasteland of the box before him looked somehow smaller and less daunting. In less than a day, it had transformed from curse to opportunity.

Chapter 21: David

David drove through the night without incident, albeit at a crawl through rough terrain. He kept his distance from battle zones to avoid detection. They shipped soldiers directly to and from the zones, so David had no knowledge of the spaces between and beyond them. He crossed the border into unfamiliar territory a couple of hours before dawn. With flatter terrain ahead of him and all the known battle zones behind him, he picked up the pace.

He hadn't driven or used old-school maps since his 20s, when all war machines were wheeled or tracked. Even in those early years, troops were mostly flown to or over front lines. With few trees or man-made structures to hide troop movements, he recalled the vehicles resembled lines of ants scurrying to the front with fresh troops and armaments and away from it with dead, wounded, or rotating troops—automatons fueled by the combustion of duty and patriotism. Still, as horrible as frontline fighting was, David preferred its geographical predictability to the ever-changing locations and daily start-stop of the battle zone missions that replaced the lines.

David was relieved the plan had worked so far, but unsure whether he could pull it off or what "it" even was. He'd spent years putting together all the moving parts for the escape. He understood it. But now he had to figure out a way home. More immediately, where was he driving to?

Heading to the port at Enirejo is a shit plan, but, for now, it's the only one I've got. It's on my 20-year-old maps, but do we still use it? Do we even use ships?

By dawn, he had navigated to a small town, which was the first civilian outpost on his route. David reckoned he could hide there during the day to rest and avoid detection. Despite advancements in sensors, AI surveillance, and night vision, he still thought daytime would make him easier to spot, imagining his vehicle as a lone moving speck in an otherwise motionless landscape.

The sun was already peeking above the horizon, so he drove just a few blocks into the settlement before seeking shelter. The encroaching sands and dust of the wasteland were overtaking the blocks of burned-out houses and crumbling roads on the edge of the town. It appeared the civilian residents had fled long ago, but he couldn't rule out a military patrol or civilian scavengers lurking in the town.

All the more reason to hunker down early and not probe too far.

David parked in the shade of the rubble of a bombed-out, three-story commercial building. The structure offered scant protection from the rising desert temps. He was plenty tired, but sleep came in fits and starts, when it came at all.

As he baked on the roof of the LAV, David hoped to find something alive in the town. A dog, a tree, maybe even a remnant survivor. He knew an abandoned town worked in favor of his escape, but he was lonely. David hadn't been allowed to interact with the controllers and couldn't relate to his fellow soldiers, but at least they offered the illusion of companionship and occasional snippets of empty small talk.

I'm trapped in an oven here and still exposed. Time to move on.

He didn't go far. The first floor of the cinderblock building was more or less intact, although two of its second-floor walls were mostly gone, exposing the interior concrete and rebar. It appeared to have been a small neighborhood grocery store, the kind that was almost extinct in the U.S. when David was a boy.

He drove the LAV through a hole where the glass entry and exit doors used to be, concealing the vehicle inside. The back seats of the LAV were comfortable enough, but even in the bowels of the ruined building, it wasn't cool. David feared that running the vehicle for the AC might alert someone to his whereabouts. He had no idea how a deserter would be treated and no desire to find out.

David woke after noon and couldn't get back to sleep. The dreams were too intense: a muddled whirlwind of childhood memories, battles real and imagined, and what the future might bring. He had had a nightmare that the box was all there was, the last bastion of mankind. A flat world where life ended at the edge of his maps.

Chapter 22: David

Waiting until nightfall to drive on seemed prudent, so David had some time for a little cautious reconnaissance. He justified the risk by telling himself he was looking for food, gear, and information that might help keep him alive, but, in actual fact, he was curious and eager to explore his newfound freedom. He'd leave the vehicle behind to minimize exposure and take his first self-directed walk outside the base.

Staying away from open areas, he kept vigilant for other soldiers, cameras, and sensors. Most of the surrounding buildings were also stores or storage buildings. No signs of life, but none expected. Just boxes and pallets and merchandise.

The town must have evacuated quickly, he reasoned, as there were no signs of looting. The store owners had just left goods where they were to gather dust or rot and decompose. Although he had vowed to remain within a few blocks of the grocery store, his reawakened sense of freedom pushed him further.

David ventured across a large, open lot to some nearby houses. The first few, surrounded by fallen or crumbling compound walls, had almost been obliterated. Armies had fought here. There was ample evidence of bullets and artillery damage. Piles of shell casings lay around berms and walls, or where walls had once stood.

The third house was surprisingly intact. It was a modest, two-story dwelling surrounded by a six-foot clay brick wall. It had a built-in single-car garage, still locked compound door and car gate, and a small yard out back. David imagined children playing and laundry drying on a laundry line that fluttered in the wind, waiting in vain for its occupants to return.

Big enough for a small family. They did well enough, but not rich. Middle class. Like me.

David hopped the wall and walked through a hole in the house into the dining room. Several plates lay on the table, with a carton of long-since evaporated milk and some now petrified eggs on a saucer in the middle. Remnants of a few food containers were strewn across the floor. In the kitchen, a dust-covered kettle perched untended on an open burner.

It was an eerie sight, sporadically backlit by completing rays of sunlight from blown-out windows and holes in the walls. A bowl sat on the floor by the backyard door.

For a cat?

Searching through the home, David found a change of children's clothes on an unmade bed, an open tube of toothpaste in the bathroom sink, and a car door left open with a briefcase open on the driver's seat. It was as if this family had been doing routine morning things and then simply vanished. No signs of a struggle, bodies, or the imagined pet cat. Nothing.

His investigation of other houses and apartments yielded similar results. A nearby park was also deserted. A baby stroller left tangled up in the chains of a swing, blown there by the wind. Cars were parked all over the street or piled up in open areas, likely pushed there by competing armies clearing lanes for their advances. A few scattered cars at an intersection had crashed into walls, lampposts, or each other.

The town was small, but sizable enough to have had a few streetlights and traffic signals. Large enough that he should have found evidence of an evacuation. It was a ghost town. A modern-day Pompeii, but without the mummified corpses.

David overlooked the ruins of the damned town from atop a four-story apartment building. Convinced the town was genuinely abandoned, he removed his helmet and scratched his wet, sweaty head in the hot afternoon sun. His mind was relieved to find it lifeless, but his lonely heart longed for human contact. Even the skeletal remains of a fellow human being would have brought him some comfort.

Having been a frequent visitor to death's door, and watched countless soldiers walk through it, David wasn't easily rattled. But this experience made his skin crawl and put his nervous tick into overdrive. The fate of the town was a new and sinister mystery. One he was ready to put behind him. David made for his vehicle and waited for nightfall.

Chapter 23: David

His body jerked back from the quicksand of sleep for the umpteenth time. He slapped himself twice and harder than before.

Come on, man. Focus!

The endless desert and lack of sleep were mesmerizing. David stuck to driving at night those first 48 hours, lights off, using his night vision. His maps served him well and, as he had planned for months, he headed toward the closest supply facility, a massive port about 220 miles from the maze.

As dawn came that second day, he was just over halfway to his destination. It snuck up on him in his exhausted state. He was reflecting on how beautiful the sunrise was when he realized he was driving in daylight. There had been no signs of life so far, and he was in a flat area far from any ghost towns. David deemed the risk to be acceptable and drove on.

He made good time that morning. The further he got from the base, its satellite battlefields, and the canyon, the better the terrain had become. Now it was flat and barren, with miles-long segments of paved road jutting out of the encroaching sandy dirt that had mostly consumed it closer to the graveyard of war machines.

The road was a remnant of a country that no longer existed. The box had long ago swallowed up both road and country. Decades-old road signs in various stages of disrepair littered the roadside in a language he couldn't read.

Every town David passed was as dead as the one he had camped in that first day. No vehicles, nothing flying overhead, no animals or even insects. David began to wonder if the port facility would also be abandoned and useless, putting an end to his escape. A dull background panic propelled him through the monotonous landscape and helped him to ignore his body's demands for sleep. He put his foot down.

The flat nothingness of the place made it otherworldly. He hummed fragments of mostly forgotten songs to stay awake. David wondered if he had died jumping off the hovercraft. Perhaps his stubborn spirit had left his corpse behind to haunt this dusty, foreboding desert, never to see his home or loved ones again.

David was careening down a particularly well-preserved stretch of highway when he saw it: water. It happened so fast that he was a good 50 yards past it and off the bridge before it registered. He screeched to a halt and slammed the LAV into reverse.

Huh?! My eyes must be playing tricks.

But, once he reversed to crest the bridge, there it was: a small stream of water. His 16-year-old map, one of his most recent, indicated it was permanently dried up. However, a few small trees and plants dotted a bank where the stream widened before going under the bridge. David retrieved his ancient binoculars and zeroed in on the largest of the nascent stand of trees.

A nest. Proof of life!

David hadn't seen life in the box or felt rain on his face for decades. But, somewhere upstream, rain had returned, and, with it, life. He scanned the area, grinning at the narrow band of green not more than eighty feet away. A few minutes later, he almost dropped his binoculars in excitement at the sight of a mother bird returning to the nest.

It was a movie he could have watched all day. Warmth in his chest replaced the fear that had possessed him earlier, motivating him to continue his mission. He drove on.

Chapter 24: David

David turned off the old highway. It was a more direct route and a less obvious approach, assuming the port still functioned. Navigating the hills and valleys required more active driving, which helped to keep him awake.

He reflected with some pride on how well he could drive, after years away from it, and more generally on how resilient he was for his age. His CivMed acquaintance had often commented that David's old body was so conditioned to trauma that he adjusted better to the demands of the battlefield than the "softer" new recruits.

His younger colleagues seemed particularly vulnerable to disruptions in sleep cycles or minor illnesses. They were raised to listen hyper-attentively to their bodies and aggressively treat every malady. David ignored pain and overcame it.

They were cut from a different mental cloth as well. Newer recruits needed step-by-step instructional videos to do anything, while David mastered tasks on his own, tailoring skills to different situations.

Troops were well cared for when they weren't on the battlefield. Overnight deployments had ceased many years ago to ensure they got enough sleep. Idle time increased markedly as the work week dwindled to three or four deployments a week. They did not have to maintain the barracks, their uniforms, or their skills. Training days were rare. All-you-could-eat buffets combined with minimal physical exercise led to expanding waistlines. All they had to do was show up for transports on time and stand where they were ordered. Less and less was demanded of them, so it wasn't surprising they demanded little of themselves.

By lasting as long as he had, breakthroughs in medical science improved David's chances of survival exponentially. Once associated with bravery and sacrifice, battlefield injuries had become mere inconveniences. Troops were patched up and turned around the same day. Within a couple hours of detecting a tumor in his throat, CivMeds had removed it with microbotic laser scalpels. That cancer would have killed him 10 years earlier. More recently, improvements stopped cancers from forming in the first place.

Lunch in the field was identical to chow at the base. Steak and lobster. Lattés on the front. The idea still seemed absurd to him, and he chuckled out loud.

"What's so funny?" Dan asked from the passenger seat.

"These cream puffs! They get fancy coffee drinks during combat now. The enemy agrees not to attack so everyone can take a full hour to eat."

"That's fucking crazy, Dave! Why don't you sneak up on them and light their shit up? Eat later."

David's eyes flashed. "That's what I said!"

"Crazy shit, Dave." Dan exhaled under his breath, looking out the window.

"What are you looking at?"

"Sensor array in front of you, barely visible up on that ridgeline. I was looking at alternate routes over there." He pointed out his window to the right.

"But that's almost going backward, at least for a while," David protested. "This is a hell of a lot faster."

"Why the hurry, soldier? Don't fuck up your great escape by going the easy way. Whores are easy too, but never worth it."

"That's what you always said, but it's still weak. Always was. Nobody thinks you're deep but your slow ass."

"I'm not slow, I'm meticulous," Dan countered. "And my slow ass says play this one safe and stay under the radar."

Back then, the troops had made fun of Dan's slow, easy-going nature. They called him Meticulous Rodriguez, a play on the cartoon character Slowpoke Rodriguez.

Today's soldiers didn't engage in that kind of banter anymore. They'd rather turn you in for it. A Slowpoke Rodriguez jest would be deemed racist and seen as creating a hostile work environment. David had been reprimanded several times for "esteem attacks" on his fellow troops, a threat to soldier confidence and unit morale. Since he had mostly stopped talking to any of them years ago, it was no longer a problem. "Humorless fucks," he muttered under his breath.

"Hey, David, you paying attention? I'm giving you good advice here and you're spacing out on me."

"Yeah, I get it. Sorry, I'm not used to doing anything that isn't texted in. No one does anything anymore, Dan, unless it comes across as an OpOrd on their readers. Nothing. No one leads from the field. Those days are over."

"Yes, they are," he sighed, suddenly more serious than the conversation merited. Something was wrong.

Of course, Dan was dead. David snapped his head back to the passenger seat. Empty now.

In his sleep-deprived state, David had imagined it all. It was all just survival instinct theater, projected by his mind. He'd conjured a familiar ghost to keep himself talking and thinking. But most of all, awake. Or was it more than that?

Whatever the case, David made the hard right turn into a valley and around a series of steep hills before turning left again, back toward his objective. It added almost two hours to his journey, but it kept him away from the sensors.

Chapter 25: David

Just as David was nodding off again, he saw it. He wasn't sure at first. It blended into the event horizon, and his aging eyes strained to see the borders. But minutes later, it was clear. He had found the port's fence.

It wasn't gleaming new but stood erect and whole. *Someone is maintaining it.*

The structure was a welcome sign of civilization after days of driving through the same light-brown, dead world. David drove within a few vehicle lengths of it before pulling to a stop. His back was killing him, and he had to unfold himself from a sitting position as he exited the car.

It was a simple chain-link metal fence with no visible cameras. Faded metal signs dotted it every 50 feet or so. "Edge of the conflict area. Do not cross. Seek guidance from a superior if lost."

David walked the fence line for a couple of hundred feet before noticing a narrow four-foot-high gap where it bent away from a support post. Ties holding the mesh sheets to the post had snapped, and the fence had partially yielded to the desert winds.

He contemplated cutting through the remaining ties up the 12-foot post to peel it back enough to drive through.

He sighed. *I'll have to climb it. I'm fuck-all tired and my back hurts.*

Contemplation abruptly gave way to a sleep-deprived anger that David directed at the barrier and at himself for overthinking it. The wire-link fence was no match for the LAV, or anything else a soldier might be driving. It was an effective barrier only as far as an encroacher respected its authority.

To hell with the fence. To hell with the faceless authorities who put me behind it and fed me bullshit orders to keep me there. To hell with their duty and honor and freedom!

As an off-grid fugitive, he was on his own now and had to make his own decisions. Decisions that might well lead him to a forgotten death, alone and unaccounted for in the desert. But he had crossed that Rubicon. Despite his exhaustion, a sense of almost euphoric rage overtook David. He started yelling at the inanimate fence as a proxy for his puppet masters.

"Do not cross, motherfucker?! Oh, I'm going to cross your ass!"

Striding over to the nearest "Do not cross" sign, David tore it from its rusted-out fence clamp, threw it on the ground, dropped his pants, and peed on it. Then he returned to the still-running LAV, backed up a bit for a running start, and gunned it at the fence until the closest metal support pole snapped at the base. The rest of the fence fell limply under his wheels.

Fear of death was a roaring fire that compelled most souls into caution and compromise. For David, that fear was now but a dwindling ember. It still sent warnings, like phantom pains from a severed limb. But he was in control now.

Let them hear. Let them come!

Chapter 26: David

The port facility was eight miles from the fence, according to David's maps, which were as much a source of information as an instrument of faith. For all he knew, the port might be twice as large now or abandoned. He crisscrossed the coastal dunes to his long-sought objective in about half an hour.

David was eager to rush straight to the port. However, his penchant for self-preservation held him back. *No, wait.*

About a mile out, he stopped the LAV on a high dune close enough to examine the port but, he hoped, far enough away to remain hidden. He parked the LAV about 40 yards from the peak and climbed to the ridge.

There it was, glowing in the morning light like the proverbial promised land: an imposing port with a dozen mile-long loading docks surrounded by a sprawling network of storage and transport facilities. A small town butting up to the other side of the complex hinted at human life, yet it appeared dilapidated and abandoned in contrast to the well-maintained port.

There were two enormous hybrid ship-submarine vessels docked. Their shiny metal hulls gleamed in the sunlight, fantastically smooth and elegant, without a straight angle to be found. Pure gold to David, for the alien-looking craft signaled the first proof of life outside his former base.

A way out! Maybe a way home?

His gaze drifted to the vast ocean feeding the port, backlit by the relentless late-morning sun. Since entering the hot and dusty box, he had often dreamt of the lakes and oceans of his youth. He gorged himself on the view, mesmerized by the waters shimmering into the infinite horizon.

David shook his head to refocus, then scanned the complex for visual activity and heat signatures. After 15 minutes, he gave up, retracted his helmet's optical system, and returned to the LAV. It wasn't invisible, but its position in a rocky dune depression and its desert camouflage veneer helped it to merge into the background. He left the helmet on the seat, strapped on his pack, and headed down the dune.

Fortunately, the dunes rolled down to the port complex, giving David decent cover until he had to bolt through 300 yards of flat, sandy soil between the last small dune and the first port warehouse. There was no fence or sign of cameras.

David caught his breath and set out to explore. The immaculate streets and structures indicated some phantom workforce was maintaining the area. Nothing was locked. Despite the rows of full and empty shipping containers, well-preserved hovercrafts, and neatly organized parts and equipment, it was dead silent and eerily lifeless.

As he approached a docking bay, David became careless, drawn like a magnet to the surrounding ocean. He emerged from his semi-concealed position along a building wall and onto the empty dock. The ocean waves beating against the dock sounded like a heartbeat. The ocean was talking to him. He no longer felt alone.

The low, grinding hum of hovercraft filled the silence between the waves. He spun back toward the complex and followed the sound two blocks forward, then one block left before he spied a convoy of shipping containers floating down a cross street three blocks ahead. His leg fully recovered, David bolted between the cover of berms and containers to stay out of sight.

The zombie-like procession of 50-foot containers drifted down the road suspended by their own power. Awaiting hovercraft positioned along the edge of the facility used spider-like mechanical arms to unload the containers. When one was packed, it launched away, and the next empty hover took its place.

Missing in all this were humans, or even robots. It was a fully automated process as far as he could tell—mechanical and cold. In about 20 minutes, the final container was loaded and deafening silence returned to the complex's vacant streets.

Where are all the people? Have they sent us all to the box?

David resumed his search, zeroing in on a tall building that appeared to be a port control tower. If this hive of soulless automation had human masters, he would find them there.

Chapter 27: David

David scaled a metal staircase along the land-facing side of the tower. The door at the peak of the stairs, about 20 floors up, had an access lock, but a wooden doorstop propped it open. David thought it was an oddly primitive tool in this modern, sophisticated facility.

It opened into a large, empty control room, which took up most of the top floor. Natural light poured in through the floor-to-ceiling glass walls on the three sea-facing walls. Desks were arrayed along holographic monitoring screens tracking shipping routes, schedules, warehouse inventories, and the like.

An almost empty cup of cold coffee perched on one of the desks, along with a stale, half-eaten pastry on a small plate. David gobbled it down, crumbs and all.

He hoped to find more food in the complex to preserve the few days of rations left in his pack.

David pushed through the swinging doors to the rear of the control room to what his angry stomach clamored for, a break room. But after minutes of rifling through every cabinet and drawer twice, he grew testy. Thumb and fingers tapped wildly as he mulled the situation. The best he could come up with was plates, flatware, cups, coffee, and some ancient, long-expired hard candies.

What did the mysterious coffee man eat? Was he an android powered by coffee?

A large steel door marked "Reserve Pantry" was locked. Every time David tried to crank the cabinet lever open, an automated voice droned, "Please provide password."

A sleep-deprived David wasn't in the right state of mind to guess the password and, after uttering a few variations of "Emergency open" and "Access food," devolved into cussing at the machine to no avail. Needless to say, "Open the fuck up!" was not the password.

Weary and hungry, he struck the wall and cried out, "All I want is some damn food!"

"What kind of food would you like?" rang out a different voice behind his left shoulder. Startled, David collected himself.

"What kind of food would you like?" repeated the voice after a few seconds, coming from a machine positioned near the sink. The push-button door was like an old microwave, but the surrounding stainless-steel machine was larger than an oven. According to its markings, it was a Food Prep 2041. David had assumed it heated food and disregarded it.

It didn't repeat its query, so David murmured, "I'd like some food, please."

"What kind of food would you like?" the voice again repeated.

"An omelet." The first thing that crossed his mind. "Yes, an omelet with ham and cheese."

"Medium, large, or extra-large portion?"

"Extra-large." Of course.

"Please insert dish." The door to the machine slid open. David fumbled around for a few seconds to find a dish and put it in.

The doors closed. "Processing ham and cheese omelet." A couple minutes later, the doors opened and trace amounts of steam rolled out, along with the smell of hot food. "Food selection completed."

David devoured the omelet, then reinserted a fresh plate for a second round. The food replicator also created drinks. The selections were limited; it didn't make fried foods, for example, but the food tasted normal enough and he was happy to have it. He wondered if it would make him a rum and Coke. No dice.

With his belly full, the need for sleep assaulted him. He had the presence of mind to clean and restack his plates and cup, which he did by hand because he couldn't figure out how to activate the automated washer. No buttons, no switches. Just magic words he didn't know.

David might have sneaked away to sleep in a less conspicuous space among the many warehouses, but he was drunk with exhaustion at this point. He dragged himself to a small, nearly empty side room with what looked like spare computer gear. David dropped to the floor, leaned his head against his pack, and fell asleep in seconds. It was early evening. David figured he'd wake long before anyone arrived in the morning. He was wrong.

Chapter 28: David

Without an alarm to stop it, David's body slept almost 11 hours. He might have slept longer, but his head fell off his pack onto the hard floor. No sooner had David regained his bearings than he noticed faint noises from the break room.

He pointed his armband in the general direction and engaged the amplifier, which directed the noise to the earpiece embedded in his ear. The sound of plates and chairs being moved. A door opening and closing. Sighs and a yawn. Then, finally, words.

"Get you a plate?" They spoke in English, though his translator would have compensated for another language.

"Yeah, grab me a cup too will ya, Andrew?"

"Hey Bernie, why do you still make your own coffee?"

"The question is why anyone wouldn't," a gravelly voice replied. "It's an art to brew the perfect cup."

"The replicator would get you the exact same thing. Healthier, too," Andrew countered.

"Just let the old-timer do it his way. It's a ritual, Andrew. The journey, not the destination. Blah, blah, blah."

"As you wish."

Conversation lulled as the men prepared their food, or, rather, the replicator prepared it for them. The soft, welcoming voice of the machine yesterday, when David had been consumed with hunger, now seemed bossy and demanding. It asked the men what they wanted and notified them when it was ready. Or was it ordering them to select food and demanding they retrieve it? It wasn't clear to David who was serving whom. David imagined the machine resenting Bernie for making his own coffee.

In the moments the men ate, David could relax and collect up his gear. He yawned, stretched out his aching back after a night on a hard floor, and reflected on something familiar about Bernie, a civilian version of himself old enough to be nostalgic about the past.

David, too, understood the ritual of coffee. Did it taste different? Was it fundamentally different from replicator brew? Maybe not, but he valued a handmade cup just the same. It occurred to him the new generation didn't value "rituals" that fed the spirit, discounting the soul as an illogical relic of superstition and religion. They discarded all that "unseen, ethereal nonsense" at the altar of science.

Sensing a kindred old fool, David yearned to walk out and introduce himself, but self-preservation overruled loneliness, as it always did.

Barely heard the man talk. Can't trust him. Could go south fast.

David's imagination raced from daydreaming about fictional relationships to paranoia. *Could they have staged that conversation?* Perhaps they knew he was in the compound and were trying to bait him into the open. He reverted to caution once again, an approach that had kept the physical husk alive all these years so the dying soul it housed might someday be saved.

No traps. I didn't come this far to blow it now.

Chapter 29: Andrew

Andrew was growing tired of Bernie's many pointless "rituals." All this "art of brewing the perfect cup" bullshit. *The old man doesn't value efficiency. Who needs art when you have science?* Plus, he had to poison the conversation with ageism, albeit self-targeted.

Smiling to himself, Andrew enjoyed the lull in their awkward chat, but he knew it would only last as long as the food. He was about to rush out after finishing his lunch when Bernie looked up from his iCom and broke the silence.

"Looks like crate loading already started for that inbound salvage transport. I tell ya Andrew, these ships run themselves anymore."

"Should be an easy job then. Good news."

"It's okay, I guess. But you're still new. After a couple weeks, you'll be bored as shit and wondering why you are out here."

"Fine by me. I've got lots of movies to catch up on. If it gets too much, I'll start a VR course."

"Anything in particular?"

"Yeah, I'm interested in the transporter tech. Hoping to get a degree."

"Makes sense. Wave of the future," Bernie said in a dismissive monotone. He stared over his cup, past Andrew.

"Appears so," Andrew echoed, not catching that this time it was Bernie who was done with the small talk.

Andrew laid out his plan. "It's a field that still isn't so automated, like shipping. I'm tired of losing my work to robots and machines. There will be a huge demand for transporter techs, at least for a while."

"Yeah," Bernie snapped. "It makes sense, but I still hate it."

"Why?"

Bernie paused, and Andrew instantly regretted the question. He reckoned Bernie was collecting his thoughts or, perhaps, deliberating whether to share them out loud. Or just old.

"All right, well, don't want to rain on your unrelenting optimism, but try to give it a bigger picture view," Bernie began.

Andrew sighed.

"They need flesh and blood people now, Andrew, so why not go for it. But one day, AI will figure out how to make and fix those transporter pods better than us, not just the technical stuff—all the way to tightening a loose bolt. Then what'll we do?"

As Bernie broke eye contact, Andrew peeked down at his iCom. Bernie likely knew he was talking to himself at that point, but he continued unabated.

"So, used to be close to 30 of us when I started, son. Now, it's just me and you and another unfilled deputy slot we don't need. And there's still almost nothing for us to do working three days a week. You may enjoy that for a while, but I suspect you'll start to feel useless. I hope you don't. Take away a man's usefulness and you might as well put a bullet in his head. Not worth anything to anyone, especially not to himself."

Andrew frowned. Free time was a blessing that allowed personkind to engage in any pursuit, relax, and spend more time with family and friends. How Bernie twisted that into something bad was beyond him. Bernie's depression was his own fault. Still, he felt a bit sorry for him.

"Sorry, Bernie. I didn't mean to create an uncomfortable working environment. Why don't you just transition out of shipping, try something new?"

"Maybe, I guess. But I've been in shipping my whole life. I captained ships; now I sit here and watch them come and go. Repairs and maintenance are rare, emergencies almost unheard of these days. I know how those old blacksmiths felt. Or lighthouse guys. I'm already a fossil, just waiting for the world to roll six feet over me.

"Anyway, enough of my pity party. You're right. Transporter tech is the way to go. Good on ya. Once that takes off, no more three-month extendable tours here. Just deploy through a portal from wherever, when and if needed." Bernie put the last "deploy" in air quotes.

"That's right! No more hardship tours," Andrew said, trying to steer the conversation back in a positive direction. "It's all so new. Exciting stuff. But I'd still rather be the guy behind the controls or fixing it than the one walking through it."

"Agreed. That's what we have the boys in the box for. God bless 'em. They'll make sure it's safe."

"I suppose so," Andrew concurred. "Their role is to sacrifice. Ours is to appreciate the freedoms they fight for."

They'd finally found some common ground, Andrew thought, but Bernie had to mention God in his morose analysis. Religious speak on the job was workplace harassment and required reporting. Policy was clear: silence is complacency.

To make it worse, "the boys" comment was sexist and inaccurate. Most troops identified as female or gender-neutral "non-binary." Andrew let both comments slide against his better judgement.

Andrew wasn't really offended and there was no one else in this forsaken waystation to take offense. No office culture or societal space to defend; it was just Bernie and him and the walls and machines of the complex. He doubted Bernie would last long once he retired and returned to the tighter scrutiny of home-front civilization, but Andrew didn't want to be the one to cancel Bernie's career and kill his pension. He also wasn't keen on filling out the forms.

"Amen," Bernie responded after a long pause.

Andrew almost let that one go, too, but couldn't resist offering an antithesis that would echo the spirit of Bernie's statement but refute the man's archaic reference with its modern replacement.

"By Goliath's wisdom," Andrew snarked with a condescending nod.

"When is the Carillion Company salvage coming in again?" Andrew asked, changing the subject.

"Yeah right, Dock 8. We should get moving." Bernie glanced down at the iCom on his forearm. "Soon, maybe 30 minutes. Ahead of schedule. Currents stronger than estimated."

"I'll get my gear and meet you there. Anything else to bring?" Andrew's chair skidded across the floor as he sprang up to escape Bernie's prognostication.

"Easy does it, young'un." Bernie raised his hand like a stop sign. "All you need is the clipboard interface. We just check a box that a human witnessed a successful docking. Then we'll come back this afternoon and check a box confirming everything was loaded right."

"Got it. Shall I wait for you, boss?"

"Go on ahead and I'll meet you down there. Not quite done eating."

Andrew nodded and rushed out.

Chapter 30: David

David barely heard the automated sliding doors swooshing open and closed as Andrew headed out. He cut the audio feed, gathered his pack, and crept out of the storage room down the small hallway to the break room doorway.

Silence. Had Bernie slipped out as well? He needed to know when Bernie left and no longer had the conversation to cue him. Taking a chance, he glanced through the window of the break room door.

Bernie's knife and fork lay neatly on his empty plate. He sat near the window, facing mostly away from David. His weathered face peeked out from a swirl of long, gray hair and beard on a short, round frame.

David imagined Bernie was taking his time, as David would have done, content to let Andrew scurry down to the already scorching hot docks and do the busy work of prepping forms. Bernie pushed his plate to the side, leaned far back in his chair, coffee in hand, and let out a deep sigh. To David, it sounded like the whimper of a wounded animal.

As David watched, Bernie's gaze shifted to the narrow gap between the wall and the table leg. He pushed his chair back, bent down, and stood up with something metal in hand.

Shit! Despite David's best efforts to leave the kitchen area as he had found it, he was tired and had forgotten to pick up a fork he had dropped while cleaning up.

David's heart raced. He grabbed his laser knife's handle from its leg strap. To ensure his presence remained undetected, he might have to kill Bernie, a prospect that turned his stomach. In the box, he had killed often, with impunity and little remorse. But this was different. Bernie was a civilian. War wasn't his job. He wasn't just another nameless soldier seeking redemption on the battlefield.

However, Bernie stared at the fork for a good while. It was on his side of the table. "Strange," he murmured. "Looks like a bit of egg stuck to it. But I don't eat eggs, and I don't think Andrew does either."

An intriguing mystery in what David imagined was Bernie's otherwise boring routine. Suddenly, an alarm buzzed from Bernie's iCom. He rose, putting the fork in the washer.

When Bernie left the break room, David waited a minute and followed. He was reasonably sure Bernie suspected nothing. David put the knife back in his leg strap, for now.

Chapter 31: David

Bernie walked from the metal platform where the stairs terminated to a hover platform. Hesitating momentarily next to the small hovercraft parked there, he walked past it, down the stairs to ground level, and onward toward the docks.

David rushed down the stairs to close the distance with Bernie and followed him to dock 8, where a slow-moving convoy of hovering containers loaded themselves into the cargo ship's hold. David jumped onto the back of a container and hitched a ride onto the ship.

Peering over the hull from a ladder that descended into the cargo hold, David watched Bernie and Andrew fiddle with their digital clipboard on the dock near the rear of the ship. As they moved and poked document holograms in the air around them, David supposed they were checking the boxes Bernie had spoken of in the break room, perhaps confirming container loads, weights, or destinations.

Bernie's enthusiastic understudy was stabbing away at the documents like a madman with a knife, while Bernie seemed to hesitate at every swipe. David assumed Bernie's slow-motion approach reflected his overt discomfort with the technology. He might have been right, but David's real motivation was to project his personality onto Bernie, a potential real-life friend for the lonely soldier. David had identified a man tired of the never-ending learning curves of new technologies with little practical benefit, at least not to him, or David.

The ease of sneaking onboard made David's brow wrinkle. He started second-guessing, or, as he would have put it, contingency planning. Was Bernie onto him?

However, that slight pang of fear, based on a hypothetical, was soon eclipsed by more real and immediate concerns. David was now a stowaway trapped in what appeared to be a massive submersible craft, running on computer autopilot. No human crew, no food, maybe no artificial oxygen supply. David had some food in his pack, but he had no idea how long the voyage would be or where it would take him. If no one knew he was on board, his next human contact might well be with a deckhand hauling his carcass out at the next port.

His head on a swivel, David began searching the decks, running through the narrow passages between tightly packed shipping containers.

Some signage on a large spiral staircase in the middle of the vessel directed him to the "bridge" above. He approached a circular manhole several floors up, roughly flush with the curved ceiling of the massive deck, which indicated he was at the highest and most central part of the ship. David slowed, wondering how he would open it with no visible levers or latches.

"Emergency bridge port opening," chirped a tinny, piped-in voice over a PA system, triggered by an unseen sensor as he neared. The spiral arms of the manhole opened and retreated into unseen housings in the ceiling, allowing David to continue through and into what appeared to be a deck of living quarters and equipment lockers for a crew. Sensors were active here too, and lights came to life as he traversed the corridors.

David's survey of the sterile, mostly empty rooms confirmed the ship was originally configured with a crew in mind, but they had long since abandoned the craft. No mattresses in the bunks and empty personal lockers. A ghost ship. Lucky for David, the last crew had failed to turn off the lights, so to speak. Climate controls and water were also operational.

Lucky, but don't jinx it, old man!

He crept gingerly into the galley, tapping his fingers nervously. David's trepidation seemed justified when it appeared cleaned out. Even the chairs and tables had been removed. As he scanned the barren cabinets for sustenance, he noticed a wall locker labeled "Emergency Rations." Sure enough, it was open and filled with vacuum-packed food pouches. The packets had expired, but they would do. He threw off his pack, sat on the floor, and wolfed down "vegan beef with gluten-free pasta #4."

As he finished his lackluster meal, he recalled his earlier encounter with the food replicator at the port mess hall. Despite its impressive technology, David might have starved had he not stumbled on the activation command in his hunger-induced rage. He much preferred this primitive setup: label food pantry, open food pantry, eat food.

David rose to his feet and mouthed "Thank you" to the heavens, reassured he had enough food for the voyage. He stared out of a port window at an infinite expanse of ocean and sky. Smiling, he imagined a bureaucratic ally that had demanded a "just-in-case" requirement to maintain emergency supplies on crewless ships. It might have saved his life.

As he emerged from the ship's mess hall, David sensed movement out of the corner of his eye down the corridor to his left. There, at the foot of a wide staircase, was Dan. He grinned and started up the staircase, motioning David to follow. David ran up the open stairs into a smaller deck perched atop the crew deck. In the event a dimwitted crew member forgot, a large "Bridge" placard was placed above an open entry at the top of the stairs. The oval-shaped room mushroomed out from the wide staircase on all sides, with workstations and control panels lining the walls. Dan was nowhere in sight.

Light poured through the wraparound windows lining the back and sides of the bridge into a massive, transparent domed portal at the front, which extended into almost half the ceiling, providing the illusion of an open deck. A traditional ship's wheel was painted on the back of an elevated captain's chair near the center of the bridge, a decorative nod to a bygone age. The craft was likely decades outdated but was high-tech and cutting-edge to David, who hadn't been on a water ship of any kind since he was 12.

Reminds me of a spaceship from an old sci-fi series.

Most of the equipment had been turned off or ripped out of the wall and probably taken elsewhere for salvage. But the main console was active, albeit with some augmented parts. Large bundles of wire connected the console to a smallish, newer-looking piece of equipment bolted to the wall above it. It was labeled "Automated Navigation System."

David speculated that the wired tentacles of this new machine invaded a more elegant system piloted by men, eliminating the roles of perhaps six or seven crew members on a shift. "Resistance is futile," he imagined the new system warning the old.

It took him about an hour to decipher a combination of screens that laid out the manifest for his journey. It would be a nearly three-day trip to San Francisco. The ship would exchange its full cargo of war scrap for a few shipping containers with base supplies in San Francisco before continuing to Guayaquil, Ecuador for an inexplicable shipment of "plant and insect generators." Then it would return to this port on the edge of the box.

As he sat in the elevated captain's chair perched near the center of the bridge, David looked up at the almost cloudless blue sky and enjoyed the sun on his face. He was nodding off when a loud, automated voice jolted him back to reality. "All hands evacuate cargo areas. Shift officers report to the bridge. Ship departure in 30 minutes. Preparing hull for anti gravity in 25 minutes." A countdown clock and anti-gravity gauges at the main console confirmed the voice's projections.

This is it.

He looked out the window behind him to where the two port hands had been checking inventories. Andrew was gone. Bernie stood motionless, staring blankly toward the vessel.

The ship's loaded and on autopilot. It's hot as hell. Andrew's gone. Why are you still standing there, you old blowhard?

David suspected it was all in his head, but Bernie appeared to be looking right at him. About 200 yards away and through the glass, David doubted Bernie could see him, but, perched high on the captain's chair in the protruding glass bridge, he felt exposed. Playing it safe, he hopped down to deck level and crouched behind a rear-facing instrument panel. A tense, possibly imagined stare-off of sorts ensued for a couple of minutes. Then Bernie gave an odd, jerky wave from just above waist level, turned, and ambled away.

Who the fuck was he waving to! Does he know? Was he righting his balance, shooing a fly, maybe waving away the ship?

David's breathing quickened as he glanced around the bridge for cameras or motion detectors. Locked in the ship, there was nothing he could do now but stew in anxiety.

"Damn that fork!" he yelled, striking his fist against his leg. "Idiot!"

David wondered if the launch would be canceled, the ship searched, and his journey unceremoniously ended. All of it for nothing. He didn't have to wait long for an answer.

Five minutes before the projected departure time, the craft began to hum. Strange sounds from the hull echoed through the ship. "Crew prepare for departure. Anti-gravity in cargo bays engaged. Wave turbines primed. On-board power at 81%. Course and currents chartered and locked. Estimated arrival adjusted to four minutes earlier than projected." Moments later, the automated voice returned to provide a 30-second countdown to departure. "… three, two, one. Launch."

For some reason, David found the voice reassuring and wondered if that was the last he'd hear of it until the ship approached its destination.

In one smooth motion, the giant vessel crouched forward and submerged simultaneously. The fact that he was going underwater in a giant submarine would have unnerved him in his younger days. But David was swept up in the magnitude of this unlikely accomplishment and feeling calmer now, with the vessel underway and vindicated in his decision to attempt escape. He had cracked no more than an occasional cynical smirk during his war years, but now he couldn't stop an ear-to-ear Cheshire Cat smile from engulfing his face. He was on the verge of pulling it off.

With nothing to do but wait, David could finally relax. Surrounded by the white noise of a ship working efficiently, he drifted to sleep in the oversized captain's chair. In a few days, he would reemerge from the dark, peaceful womb of the ocean to be reborn in his birth country after so many years divorced.

His subconscious searched for a dream about coming home. But he had no reference to its present state. Instead, David imagined his home and family from before the endless war, because that was all he knew.

Unnoticed by David, one of the control room screens flickered. A message in simple text appeared: "Safe travels." Bernie knew.

Chapter 32: Jane, Mary, and Kor

Jane awoke. No alarm and no idea what time it was. She stretched a bit, rolled over, and tried to go back to sleep.

Whether waking or dreaming, Jane fought the false utopia imposed on her with dreams of a genuine, imperfect world that ought to exist in its place. Her resistance was the only thing she could control. It was existential. Retreat wasn't an option.

Yet, she was retreating from the modern world in unconscious ways. Inward. She had become the center of her world and that was a lonely place to be.

Across town, her sister Mary awoke as her sleep monitor sensed her fourth circadian rhythm coming to an end. She never deviated from her optimal sleep pattern. Mary didn't need an alarm, but she liked the affirmation it provided. It told her she was waking up when she should.

Mary sprang from her bed. Her meal and coffee timers chimed in unison as she entered the kitchen, welcoming her. She ate a light breakfast before engaging in her morning yoga. Body sensors tracked her progress and vitals.

This was Mary's "me time," but her thoughts, as usual, drifted to her husband and children, who would soon wake. Every morning, she gratefully plotted how to best exploit the bounty of time and opportunities the world, her family, and her friends afforded her. She was blissful, and blissfully unaware.

◄◇►

On the other side of the continent, Kor had been up for hours. His sky sled crested the skyscraper and navigated through the trees of a small rooftop park. Kor hopped off as the craft slowed to a halt outside the Council of the Americas. Seconds later, it sped away to another rider in parts unknown.

It was an oddly small conference hall, considering the magnitude of the decisions made within its humble wooden walls. There was no sign outside its arched entrance to herald its importance. No guards. No media. No public.

Elites gathered here to decide the fate of United America. They needed no grandiose structure to compensate for insecure egos or impress their constituents. There was no reason to appeal to them, as the councilors' power was absolute and indefinite.

Kor squinted over the horizon of the city as his ocular implants adjusted to the bright morning sun. It was an impressive view: a blur of emerald greens mixed with the pastels and grays of the buildings that made up the modern metropolis before evaporating into the blue ocean beyond. Rivers of hovercraft flowed between structures on invisible paths, some moving people, others moving products. The Goliath Network ensured peaceful, seamless traffic.

Birds chirped and sang above the almost silent hum of the emission-free hovercrafts. A rich oxygen blanket engulfed the city, provided by the plants that crawled over its horizontal and vertical surfaces. Pollution and gray cityscapes only existed in Kor's earliest memories, anchoring a subconscious appreciation every time he breathed in city air that tasted as fresh as mountain air. The morning sun cast a spotlight on the splendor of a reborn New York and a warm beam of sunshine on Kor's bearded, angular face. He took in the view and wondered whether he was right to suggest changing this paradise.

He was generally solitary, like Jane, but concerned himself with the welfare of others, like Mary. That concern meant he seldom slept as well as Mary, but it also saved him from the nocturnal anxiety of Jane, who only ever dreamed about her insecurities and fears.

As was the norm for the times, Kor had never married. He was an only child and had a strained relationship with his oligarch parents, who disagreed with his politics. Kor felt little more than a fleeting connection with a few extended family members. No one would guess he was a godparent to four children from three sets of parents, a role he relished and performed admirably. Although not his own, those children gave him reason enough to care about the future, right wrongs, and plot a better future.

But it was a hard fight. The council would meet today to, once again, hear his arguments. They would likely, once again, agree to table his motions for a more suitable time.

Such a body sworn to reason, compassion, and global stewardship could not easily ignore Kor's irrefutable truths or altruistic vision. However, even the members who agreed with him were in no hurry to rush the process. Such dramatic changes needed to be thought through and perfectly executed, lest they threaten hard-fought gains and lead mankind, once again, to the brink of extinction.

But the concept of "perfect" was a human one, and waiting for the perfect plan and the perfect time effectively meant waiting in perpetuity. Kor's vision could not be ignored in good conscience, but it could be slow-rolled under the guise of caution. And it was.

Yet, Kor was undeterred. Clenching his fists, he entered the chamber to argue once again to free the human race from its warm cocoon of ignorance. He understood the need for deception, but with the crisis behind them, he saw no compelling reason to continue it.

Free from electoral timelines and public scrutiny, the council had largely taken the opposite approach, arguing there was no need to change the status quo. As Kor knew, lurking in the back of their minds lay a base fear of their subjects that even he shared. Given fruit from the tree of knowledge, they might well choke on it.

Chapter 33: David

"You are approaching Seattle Main Station."

The automated voice pulled David grudgingly from sleep. He sat up and rubbed his eyes, feeling the checkered pattern of the seat's headrest temporarily tattooed across his face and forehead. The transport slowed as it descended into port along the towering buildings of Seattle. The night hid much of the jet city outskirts in darkness, but he recognized the illuminated space needle in the distance and an occasional park or building. Familiar, yet alien.

David had tried to stay awake so he could relive his childhood trips between San Francisco and Seattle. The magnetic rail followed much the same path as the old ocean highway his family had happily slumbered down for a full day in long-extinct automobiles. Now, the maglev transport he was on barreled down the electron-charged track at speeds so fast he could barely make out the distant horizon, let alone the scenery in front of him. The entire trip was scheduled at just under two hours, and only because the transport made several stops.

Before boarding a transfer headed to his hometown, David overheard a young girl at the Seattle station complain to her mother about how slow the maglevs were. The girl mentioned a new technology that would allow them to transport over enormous distances in seconds. They were both inadvertently mocking David's awe of the "old" transports. It made him realize how long he'd been gone and how much had changed.

It was so easy to get here. Free transportation, free food. Everything is easy here.

David collected his thoughts. After the ship docked in San Francisco the night before, he'd snuck out while the containers unloaded themselves. If any living person was on the docks, he didn't see any evidence of them.

Keeping to the shadows where possible, David had headed toward town. There was no discernable surveillance. No one was walking around the empty port streets. He panicked a bit, wondering if the city was just another abandoned ghost town, like those he had encountered in the box. An occasional transport hummed by, reassuring him someone was piloting them, remotely or not. His last semblance of human contact had been with the dock workers, Bernie and Andrew. He yearned for more evidence of human life.

He'd soon found it. The modern industrial area around the port transformed into a residential area. The dilapidated, vestige pavement of the docks gave way to pedestrian pathways where roads once existed, surrounded by park-like landscaping. Otherwise, the subdivisions seemed comfortingly like David's memories.

No one stirred in the still, dark houses. No late-night partying or loitering kids this chilly night. The doors had digital readouts that told passersby the exact location of the residents. At the third house, he noted the residents were in Mexico. Surprisingly, house lighting and doors switched on and opened as David approached. Nothing was locked. He took advantage.

The house was opulent, with wall-to-wall screens projecting art, calendars, and broadcasts. He learned he could change the configuration of most of the interior walls. Upon entering most rooms, automated voices offered services. The kitchen asked if he wanted anything to eat or drink, while the living room offered to change the lighting and played music "based on prior preferences." Overwhelmed by choices, David asked to watch the news.

A broadcaster filled the wall he faced. When he moved, the video followed him through the house, even projecting onto the ceiling and floor, depending on where he was looking. The newscast focused on celebrities, entertainment, new devices, and the weather. It did little to help David understand how to navigate the world beyond the box. Tired and disappointed, he asked the house to turn it off after a few minutes.

To his delight, one of the vacationing residents was his size. David picked out gear he'd need for the onward journey, ate, showered, and collapsed into a bed that suspended him in the air, as if he was floating in space. The residents weren't due to return for days, so he felt secure enough to sleep without an alarm.

David slept until just before noon the next day.

"Show me how to get to Seattle," he asked. The house's technology projected a map and directions.

"Would you like me to download it to your iCom?"

"No, no thank you." David sighed in embarrassment for showing the house human politeness. With a series of similar requests, the house plotted David's journey, which he committed to memory.

For the first time, he traversed the thoroughfares of his homeland, a strange and wondrous place full of pedestrians, many out for a morning walk or run. Hovercraft hummed along above them.

David was amazed, but he resisted the temptation to gape at the sights around him. Eventually, he succumbed to his loneliness and struck up a few conversations. People were relaxed and friendly enough, yet they frowned at David's short, choppy sentences and long pauses; the syntax of a person decades removed from regular conversation.

And so, his research began. Despite remnants of the past still lingering in pockets of San Francisco, it wasn't the city he remembered. Just beneath his confusion and curiosity, anger boiled. As David compared this home-front paradise with the hell of the box, he clenched his teeth so hard he feared breaking them. Questions surged through his cortex.

What happened to my country? *What happened to my hometown? My home?*

He would find out soon enough. The final transport came to an abrupt stop, pulling him back into the present and completing the journey to his hometown. The pod door opened above him. David walked out of the terminal to a pick-up and drop-off area across from a small park.

I know that park.

The old post office, now a museum, still stood at the far end. All the other buildings around it appeared new, at least to him.

David expected the small town to have grown, but he was unprepared for the magnitude. He found it unsettling. At one point, he caught himself putting his arms up in a fighting stance, as if under attack from the urban growth that was suffocating the defenseless old buildings with soulless modern structures.

Commuters had their noses in their iComs and were hopping in and out of personal hovercraft transports of all sizes at the "bus terminal," apparently a vestige term as he saw nothing that looked like a bus anywhere. There was little chit-chat. No one lingered. About five minutes after the 10 PM transport arrived, the last of the day, the city center had emptied itself, fully lit but devoid of the merry social scene it had generated when he was young. Not a drunk, or a cop, or a vagrant to be seen.

He assumed the hovers would only work for people wired with iComs. Even if he could start one, he feared being tracked and identified. David suspected he would draw attention to himself by walking around at night and showing up at his old home around midnight. He determined the prudent course would be to stay the night in the deserted park and rest up for the day ahead.

David slept a few hours on a park bench before beginning the long pre-dawn walk to his parents' family farm, uncertain of what he'd find there, or if it would even still be there. Just under eight miles on foot, but a million miles from his memories.

Chapter 34: Frank and Judith

It was a weekend, but the Sanders family woke early, anyway. The farm hadn't had a cow on it for decades, but they adopted the rural routine of early rising simply by living on the old place. Its character infected them.

When faced with the decision to raze the farmhouse or remodel it, they kept it. Frank was retiring and liked the idea of doing most of the work himself. He was an outlier; vocations involving physical labor were almost entirely automated now and only nostalgic hobbyists engaged in home repair.

Frank had spent his career "working in the phantom zone," as he put it. He refined computer systems, where nothing he did was tangible or, in his eyes, real. He sent data in the form of electrons out to some unknown destination in virtual reality and received electrons back, mostly from people he didn't know—people he couldn't even prove existed. It was like being on a deserted island in cyberspace, sending out virtual messages in electronic bottles to other stranded fellow travelers on their own islands. Years of virtual work had rendered them distant from each other, whether they were self-aware enough to realize it or not. Virtual was real enough for most, but not for Frank, who felt it transformed him into just another bundle of electrons caught in the Network's digital web.

The "do-it-yourself" ethos Frank remembered from his youth no longer existed by the time he wanted to give it a try. To find how to build things himself and remodel his home in particular, Frank had to dig deep behind the Network's more popular information.

But he had the time and was thrilled to create things "with his own two hands." His neighbors thought him crazy and, from their vantage, he probably was. While they "enjoyed" their free time, Frank filled his tinkering with imperfect home improvements better tasked to flawless robots and machines.

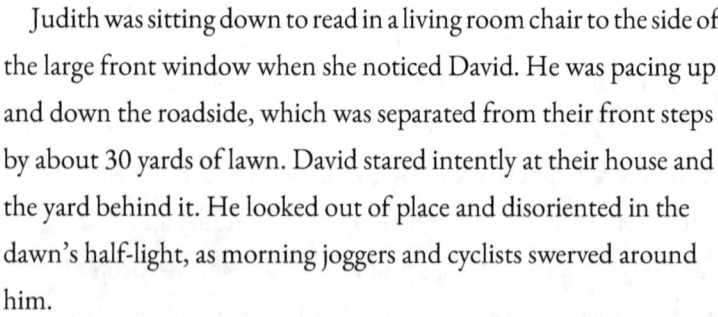

Judith was sitting down to read in a living room chair to the side of the large front window when she noticed David. He was pacing up and down the roadside, which was separated from their front steps by about 30 yards of lawn. David stared intently at their house and the yard behind it. He looked out of place and disoriented in the dawn's half-light, as morning joggers and cyclists swerved around him.

She read for a few minutes. When she looked up, he was gone, only to reappear minutes later. When she called out to Frank, who emerged yawning from their bedroom, he was gone again. She went back to her book (a double throwback as few people read anymore, and only "oldbook" eccentrics did so from the printed page).

After stretching out some morning kinks, Frank wandered back to their bedroom, which they shared. Almost no one shared a bedroom or a bed these days. It was considered unconducive to sleep and public health, and a bit of a dirty old habit. Judith knew it opened them to ridicule, but she enjoyed feeling Frank fling his arm over her in the middle of the night and hearing his slight snore as she nodded off to sleep. To her, it sounded like a contented, reassuring purr.

Chapter 35: David

David's stomach churned. It was his family's old house, all right. It looked much the same from the outside, but it had been gutted and rebuilt judging from what he could see through its windows. David found such modern curtainless glass houses excessively transparent, offering too much information about their occupants to the world and the Network.

The surrounding farm, with its gentle rolling meadow and red barns, had also vanished. A bevy of modern homes and apartments filled those eight acres. The town had swallowed his childhood whole.

He walked around the block and found it much the same. An occasional home, road, or canal anchored in his memory confirmed he was in the right place, but the future had stolen the rest and left a new, foreign suburban utopia. He shivered.

The once-familiar walk from the center of his once-small town to his childhood home was also disorienting. Luckily, the route was seared into his subconscious, and he found his way home through muscle memory.

A vein throbbed in David's neck as he regarded the unfamiliar woman behind the window. He was trying hard not to hate her. It was illogical to expect his parents to still be living there, much less alive, but he'd still held out hope.

Instead, he'd found interlopers squatting in his old home. David waited until a reasonable time in the morning to knock on the door so he wouldn't alarm the new residents, not realizing technology had rendered that analog greeting unnecessary. An automated doorbell rang as he approached the front door.

"Good morning. How are you?" he muttered, shifting from foot to foot. No one offered such quaint niceties in the military, but he had rehearsed his greeting for hours, pulling the sayings from the recesses of his pre-war recollections. Unfortunately, they were dated, just like David.

"How am I?" Judith stammered. "None of your business. What do you want?"

"Sorry." He flushed. "I didn't mean to offend. I don't care how you are. It's just something we used to say when I was a kid. I've been gone a long time."

Judith sensed the genuineness in David's reproach. She was old enough to remember such polite banter. However, it was considered phony now. "It's okay. So, what brings you here?"

"I used to live in this house, back when it was a farm. I'm looking for my parents."

"Oh, well, that's a while back. Your mom sold it to us about 10 years ago, when she couldn't keep up with it. She moved into a new place not too far from here. That cluster of senior residences out by the lake. It's not far."

Mom's alive?! David dug his fingers into his palms to keep from shouting to the heavens. With a deadpan expression, he nodded. "Thank you."

Judith gave David the names of the cross streets. He was almost on his way and Judith back to her book when Frank hurried out of the kitchen to the door wearing a stern frown and the demeanor of a protective pit bull.

"Hold on there!" Frank wedged himself into the space between his wife and David. "Why can't you look this up yourself?"

David fell silent. He'd lost the ability to maintain conversations beyond the soldierly "Yes, sir" and "No, sir." Besides, Frank was right.

"I, uh, missed an upgrade, need an upgrade," David stammered. "Can't log on."

"Can't log on? Everyone can. There's no choice to it. That sounds like horse shit!"

"Smells like horse shit, dear," Judith chimed in. David sensed she was trying to defuse the standoff, but her ear-to-ear grin belied a pleasure at her husband's clumsy heroics.

"Yes, whatever." Frank was undistracted. "Well, I don't know what you're up to, but I don't like it. You need to leave."

"Yes sir," David said reflexively. "I thank you. I'll deploy immediately."

"Go on now." Frank folded his arms. "Lucky I don't know how to report this."

Lucky indeed, David thought as he marched off the patio, wondering how Frank didn't know how to call the cops and hoping he wouldn't figure it out.

Chapter 36: Judith

Judith's eyes gleamed. The stranger was a mystery. As soon as David had walked down the hill and out of sight, she pulled up her forearm iCom to document the incident on her profile. Such a bizarre and vaguely dangerous encounter was sure to generate likes and comments.

What will they all say? They won't believe it! They'll send it on.

With the ratings boost, Judith would finally break out of her low 80s score, where she'd lingered since they moved to the small, uneventful town. But halfway into her entry, she realized how embarrassing it would be to admit that the scruffy no-goodnik had fooled her. She'd almost invited him in. Her husband had to come to her rescue, a sexist trope that would not trend well. Sighing, she deleted the post she'd labored on for an hour.

Ratings were tracked on the Merit Indicator, or MI—pronounced "Me" for short because it was synonymous with the identities of Network users. It was the ultimate measure of a person's worth; in essence, a digital Santa doling out social merit carrots and sticks accordingly for deserving and undeserving behavior.

Thanks to the complex system of iComs and tracking devices, anyone hooked up to MI could expect a rating drop for a traffic infraction or eating a pizza, and a boost for returning the shopping cart or exercising. No action was too small or too insignificant.

Without implants, David was perhaps the only person in the country the MI couldn't track. Thankfully, the MI only recorded public actions, which allowed people to remain more genuine and unguarded in private. Private space laws guaranteed them a reprieve from the surveillance state. In theory.

Chapter 37: Gale

Gale's home notified her of an "unknown person at the door."
That was odd. The doorbell always knew who was at the door. She
assumed it was a glitch in someone's tracker or a stray cat.

She opened the door and found a muscular, older man with a
weathered face and a trembling, outstretched hand poised to knock.

Blinking, she tried to place the face. But once they locked eyes,
vivid memories of her dead son flashed over her consciousness like
a neural hurricane. "YOU'RE HOME!" she shouted and reached
out, unwittingly drawing David into the first human embrace he'd
had since he was a young man. "My boy," Gale muttered through
her sobs, repeating the phrase over and over.

Chapter 38: Mary

Mary and Jane received the same short, frantic holographic alert from Gale to come straight to her house. She said David had returned. But David was dead.

After rereading the message for the third time, Mary called Jane. Instantly, her sister's holoimage appeared.

"What the fuck, Mary. Did you read it?"

"Yes, I don't understand it, but I don't want to overreact. Do you think Mom means 'returned' in a figurative sense? Or maybe she's created a mural or holographic display of some kind?"

"Dunno. Hope you're right. I was thinking maybe she took a nap, had a vivid dream about David, and took it as real."

"No idea. She's shown no signs of dementia—zero. She still beats my kids at board games and knows more about things than anyone in the family."

"Anyone?"

"Jane, you need to take this seriously."

"I am. But come on! She's almost 100 years old. I know that's the new 50 and all, but science still hasn't found a cure for mortality."

Mary pursed her lips. "Jane, I don't like talking about Mom that way. Let's just get over there and see what's what. If it's cognitive, we can get an implant."

"Well duh, of course we'll go over. And check your tone," Jane grumbled. "You act like I don't care because I'm not on a virtue signal hair trigger. And you start every sentence with my name like you're talking to your kids!"

Mary took a deep breath. She didn't like the passive-aggressive virtue signaling reference but didn't want to escalate. Plus, Jane wasn't wrong. Mary did talk down to her sister as if she were a child, even if she often acted the part.

"Right, okay, sorry. I'll meet you there."

"Yeah. And expect a fight on implants. I wouldn't want one either."

"Well, let's see if it goes that way. Maybe it was just a misunderstanding. You'll get there first; I've got to figure out what to do with the kids."

"I know. Don't worry about it. And I won't steer Mom in any direction until you get there."

"Thanks." Mary paused for a split second. "Love you."

But Jane had already hung up. Their relationship had been particularly tense the last few months. Mary hoped whatever her mom's issue was, it might provide an opening to patch things up with her renegade sister. They could help their mother deal with David's death together, once and for all.

Chapter 39: Mary

Mary sat on the couch with Jane, watching in disbelief as David and Gale combed through old photos. It amazed her how fast Gale had reassembled herself around the wonderful truth of David's return.

Her mother's identity was so wrapped into being the parent of a slain hero that Mary wondered who Gale would be now. But it was soon clear that any lingering reservations on her mother's part had given way to the overwhelming joy of having her David back. She skipped frantically between asking David questions, telling him about the years he had missed, and gazing at him in wondrous appreciation. Gale unleashed a flurry of intermittent hugs, pats, and kisses between the words. For his part, David seemed in a blissful, shell-shocked trance as he accepted the assault of affection. Few sentences were finished. Many questions were left unanswered.

Mary smiled when Gale ran her withered hands over David's scarred, battle-worn face. When Gale whispered, "I missed you," Mary mouthed "Me, too." But as much as she wanted to enjoy the moment, Mary couldn't drop her skepticism. This was, after all, an impossible reunion. Disbelief gnawed at her.

After about an hour, Mary started coming to terms with the new reality. She wanted to believe, after all. She asked David to join her outside to check on the grill.

"So, how do you feel?" Mary asked, openly staring. Unable to stop herself.

"Fine. Tired, otherwise fine."

"That's not what I mean," Mary said as she turned the skewers. She found the conversation easier if she didn't have to look at David. "What's it like to be back?"

"A little overwhelming." He sighed. "I can't believe I'm here, and yet, I'm not really sure what here is anymore."

"Yes, lots of changes, lots of changes." Mary wanted an excuse to keep talking but was unsure what to say. "Are you hungry?"

"Yes, so hungry." David stared down at the grill, all vegetables. "But where's the hamburger? The meat? What kind of barbecue is this?"

Mary smiled. "Hamburgers? Well ... right ... It has been a long time. I don't know what they are feeding you on the front lines, but we haven't had burgers since, well, almost as far back as when we were kids."

"Do you miss them?"

"No, I never think about it, actually."

"We don't."

"Don't what?"

"Eat burgers, in the field, I mean. I thought of it because of memories. Of how Dad used to grill. Don't grill in the field, or talk much. Sorry if not clear."

"How did you get back?" Mary looked up at him as she pushed a button to close the grill's lid.

"I ... don't know what to say. Where to begin," David stammered.

Mary had noticed a distinct change in tone and cadence. *Is he struggling to explain it or does he not want to? He was just reveling in his rediscovered family, and I set him off. He seems so ... pained.*

"What happened to Dad?" David countered. "He's gone. That's all I know. Mom just talks around it when I ask."

Mary wasn't sure what to make of David changing the subject to talk about their mom doing the same thing. In the living room, he had changed his train of thought constantly, sometimes in mid-sentence. Was he simply unable to maintain a normal discussion, damaged from the war, or was he hiding something?

Gale saved both David and Mary from those tough conversations when the sliding door flew open and she peeked out, her eyes shining with impatient pleasure.

"David, please come in, dear. I want to show you photos of your nieces and nephews. Come, come." Gale motioned for David to return.

Mary's jaw tightened. She supposed it was harmless enough to show David images of her kids, but she wasn't ready to introduce him to them.

She voiced a quick message to Jane, but then remembered her sister didn't have an ear implant to hear it and converted it to text instead: "Don't let her rope my kids into this!"

David wasn't really David anymore, and she needed to figure out who was inhabiting the body of her brother, long thought deceased.

Explaining it to her kids would have to wait until she understood it herself.

Mary would need to be sure about David, but she was starting to succumb to the happy possibility that he was somehow alive. Sitting down on a nearby chair, Mary watched the others through the sliding glass door, her shoulders relaxing for the first time since arriving.

She smirked at the mention of showing David "photos," a quaint term for another technology long forgotten. Her mother clung to the old ways and sayings. Like her ornamental doorbell. Like her insistence that her son was still alive, a fire Mary thought had long since been extinguished but was now back with a vengeance. Some of that fire was awakening in Mary as well.

Chapter 40: Gale

The next morning, Gale awoke as the sun cascaded through her bedroom window, illuminating the room in a warm glow. It was fall and normally she would be up at dawn. But this time, she'd slept in, which was unusual enough to startle her. She sat up in bed, touching the base of her neck.

Why's it so late?!

Then it all came flashing back. David had returned. He wasn't dead. He'd appeared out of the blue yesterday afternoon. Much older. It had taken Gale a good five seconds to see her son under the weathered skin and graying hair, and a further hour to fully accept it.

There had been a mistake at the war bureau. Her son was alive! Living, breathing, and sitting at her kitchen table.

Once she'd started to accept her fantasy might be true, she'd called her daughters to join them. There were joyful but awkward hours during this reunion as disbelief and shock melted away into the night. David's death had pushed the family apart in many ways. Now his return was pulling it back together, it seemed.

It had taken Gale years to accept David's death. Even then, a sliver of hope glowed in the unseen shadows between her heart and mind. There was no body. Even though the war bureau had stopped shipping back remains soon after the war began, she still held out hope. After six grief-stricken years of denial and at the persistent advice of well-meaning friends, she'd visited his grave, symbolically surrendering to the cold fact of her son's passing.

But it wasn't true. David was alive. She had been right all along!

Or had she? Now fully awake, heart racing from the startling recollections, Gale wondered if she had dreamt it all. Was the late night the explanation for her late waking or had she just succumbed to a wonderful dream? She hastened from the bedroom to confirm for sure.

There, sitting at the kitchen table, once again, was the man who'd turned her world on its axis yesterday. The harsh morning light shrouded him, backlighting his figure like a stained-glass window against the greens and browns of the garden on the other side of the window. She focused. It was David.

"It's true," she whispered. She'd meant to say it in her head, but it was too important not to escape verbally.

At that moment, David turned to face her. "Good morning, Mom."

Chapter 41: David

Gale's eyes gleamed as she showed David all the treasures she'd saved from his childhood. Her garage was a museum of boxes stacked deep and high with David's things—one with his old Boy Scout projects, another with school projects and horrible short story attempts (Gale thought he'd be the next Steinbeck), and another couple of boxes with comic books, fishing poles, BB guns, his prom suit, and clothes.

He was relieved he still fit in some of his old clothes, as the fashions of the day were both foreign and unappealing to him. People wore bland, similar-looking, one-piece outfits in blue, brown, and black pastels that made crowds look like amorphous blobs. Nanite-bonded material changed density and size based on temperature. Functional, practical, boring. After almost half a century in the military, he'd had enough of wearing uniforms, whether imposed or self-imposed.

"Look, son," Gale cried. "Your old skis. Perfect timing. They just started skiing again a few years ago."

Gale explained the snow had simply stopped coming shortly after he left. A couple of years ago, it started returning as temperatures dropped.

"Now it piles up the way it used to and stays a full season without any help from snow-making machines."

His mother started pulling out his ski boots from a high shelf. She was talking about planning David's ski reunion with old friends. Suddenly, the side door to the garage flew open and ricocheted off the wall. Mary darted in and looked around wildly before spotting them in the back.

"Run!" she cried, gasping for breath. "People are here! Gathering outside. Trying to get you! Run, David! Run!" She pivoted out of the way and pointed at the door to the hallway behind her. "Down the hallway! Back door, back door! Go! Go!"

Just like that, David was back in the box. His survival instinct took over. He sprinted past Mary and down the hallway without looking back. He heard the front door thrown open behind him.

The back door was glass and led to the deck. Standing behind it was a tall, young man in a black, vaguely military uniform. His eyes bugged when he saw David. He had begun to move his hand toward his belt holster when David crashed through the glass door, knocked him down, and sprang over the deck into a small, grassy backyard that emptied into a suburban alley.

David spied two more uniformed officers down the far end of the alley to the left. They stiffened, then snapped to attention and ran to close the 30 yards between them. David bolted to the right.

No one in sight. He ran like hell, plotting his next move as he neared the end of the alley and the main road beyond. Just as he broke into a full stride, David spied a transponder off to the side. Too late to keep himself from smashing into a transparent electric net. It knocked him out instantly, and he collapsed to the ground with a thud.

Escape thwarted. Once again at the mercy of others who would plot his destiny.

Chapter 42: Jane

"How could you?" Mary snarled. She was alternately wiping her eyes and stabbing her finger at her sister, which made it appear as if she was hurling tears at Jane like lightning bolts.

"How could I not?!" Jane was trying hard to appear unaffected to minimize the consequence of her actions. Despite her cool facade, Jane's emotional scaffolding was buckling inside. She had, after all, just ratted out her brother.

"It had to be done," she rationalized. "You know it's against the law not to turn him in. It's called harboring a fugitive, Mary."

"It's called turning in your brother!" Mary snapped.

"Really? Are you kidding me?!" Jane reverted back to a time when schools had debate teams, and she was her team's president. She was on autopilot now, lobbing counterarguments to justify her decision—not really believing any of them. "Mary, the one who always does the right thing, is telling me this? You've got kids. Thank Goliath they'll never meet David!!"

The two sisters were recovering from the morning's events, having just calmed their mother enough for her to lie down. They sat at the far end of the balcony, the furthest point from Gale's bedroom, so as not to disturb her.

"You're bringing my kids into this? Fine," Mary replied, taking deep, slow breaths. "Yes, I want my kids to obey the rules, but I also want them to live in a world they can question. A world where they are a little less about themselves and a little more about others. About the uncle they never knew! Our brother!"

Jane snorted. "Oh Mary, really? This uncle you speak of. Do you know him as well as you think? Can you even be sure it's David after all these years?"

"Yes, oh yes! I know it's David and so do you!" She looked Jane square in the eyes. "Tell me that wasn't David! Come on!"

Jane struggled to reply. Her rational arguments evaporated against a question that called for emotional judgement. Not what she thought, but what she felt.

"I, well, it certainly ..." she stopped, inhaling slowly. "I think it was David, but I also have to report him, right?"

"No, it was a choice. You made the call without us. We could have waited, found out more!"

Desperate to regain the upper hand, Jane let some bitter truth slip out. "You could have waited, Mary. But you've got a, got a s-sky-high rating!" Jane's speech suddenly became staccato and choppy.

"What if I waited and it turned out badly? I've got nothing; it would wipe me out. I can't afford to have principles or feelings. Look where it got me!" With that, hardcore Jane broke into a blubbering cry, barely able to get the last part out coherently, and collapsed on a nearby deck bench.

There was no margin of error if you had a rock-bottom rating, as Jane did. The system wouldn't let you starve, but there was a social and practical price to being low-rated. Good ratings afforded you the latest tech, access to events, better healthcare, and prime housing. Potential friends and lovers judged you on it.

Jane was a talented writer, but no one would follow her work because of the points drop they would get for reading it. Freedom of speech endured in theory, but it was only exercised in any meaningful way by the popular.

"Yes, I can understand that," Mary said. "I've been rewarded for good behavior my whole life. But I was living the life I would have, anyway. There was never any daylight between my values and the system. Until now."

Noticing a pause, Jane peeked up from her sobbing to find Mary waiting to lock eyes.

Her sister continued. "You're not the only one who struggled with the David situation. Maybe I'll be held complicit for not calling him in, warning him instead. But I love him. I'd do it again!"

After that cathartic introspection, Mary sighed and sat down on the same bench. "I know it seems like I love the system, Jane. That I'm blind to its faults. But I'm not! I hate how it mistakes what's popular for what's right."

Jane nodded, taking shaky breaths as she regained her composure. She wasn't used to letting others talk this long without interrupting, but she allowed Mary to vent unchallenged.

"But thinking on it," Mary continued, "I'm not sure I care anymore. Having a lot of social capital should mean less worry, but you just have further to fall. More to lose."

Jane noticed Mary had fully geared down from antagonist to confidant, revealing to Jane an inner conflict she knew her sister would understand and not judge her for now.

"I never thought about it much. Now I'm doubting everything. I was up all night wondering why we all thought David was dead when he wasn't. We had no proof, Jane! We just believed what they told us. Mom rejected it for years, but that was the emotional reaction of a mother. You never believed it because you didn't trust the system, full stop."

"But I also didn't want to believe it because I loved him, too!" Jane retorted, trying to show her sister that she, too, was more than Mary believed her to be. That she too had an emotional stake in the matter. A soul. "I'm not a robot, Mary!"

She left it at that but, as soon as she said it, she asked herself if maybe she had become one. She wanted to tell Mary about the hundreds of hours of research she had done to prove Goliath lied about David, about all the evidence she'd amassed. Too dangerous to reveal. In that moment, she fell through a trapdoor of despair, trying to reconcile what she'd done to prove David was alive, only to turn on him when it turned out she was correct.

Worse than a robot, I'm a monster.

"Of course, of course," Mary said, snapping Jane from her downward spiral. "But you also looked at it rationally, as always. Maybe you could see it for what it is. We were all too gullible.

Something's not right here and David proves it. I thought you were just cold and self-interested, but I was wrong."

"You call it self-interest. It's survival! That's all it's ever been for me," Jane cried. "Altruism is just a way selfish people get to feel better about themselves. I'm selfish. I should have ..." She trailed off in self-doubt, assailed by a bevy of would'ves, should'ves, and could'ves regarding her decision to turn in David.

Jane was no longer reflexively pushing back against her sister's assault. She was pushing inward, questioning herself and her world.

True to her compassionate nature, Mary reached out and took her sister's hand. "Jane, I understand. You had a lot to lose. But this isn't you. You are the rebel, the person who stands up to the system. I didn't like that person all the time, but I don't want to lose her either. What's done is done, but don't let it so totally change you."

Mary's unexpectedly kind words provided a beacon for Jane to escape her dark guilt. Jane cracked a hopeful smile back and looked skyward, dislodging a tear that slid down her cheek.

Her sister drew her closer and enveloped her in a long hug. They could agonize about it to eternity and back, but David was gone. Nothing could change that. All they could do was forgive one another. And find David.

Chapter 43: Mary and Jane

Mary cared more about others than herself. Given that this particular other was her ostensibly deceased brother, her allegiance to him was never in doubt.

Despite her professed love of intellectual pursuits, Jane was self-centered and driven by ego. What she would have proudly called an individualist. Now both she and her sister were questioning those roles and moving into each other's space.

The conversation had turned the conformist into the rebel and the rebel into the conformist. Their shared affection for their brother, David, had cleared a path of introspection they now walked together. His arrival had torn down the invisible walls of their status quo assumptions, leaving them both reeling.

When the ground shifts beneath your feet, your first instinct is to survive. After that, you are left to contemplate what has happened and why. New ideas can creep into that space, since, by definition, the unexpected is beyond what old thinking can explain. That's the place where people can change their minds, even about themselves.

From the Author

Many decades ago, I was a soldier. My unit was slated for war zone deployment. Although we never went, I studied the causes of the conflict and our proposed involvement. I found both wanting. It weighed on me. It seeped into my dreams. Those dreams became this story.

In recent years, I happened upon my original hand-written novel. Its dark prognostications of forever wars, resource scarcity, democracy, and technology became more prescient and urgent with time. I updated it with contemporary manifestations of these anxieties, including AI, social media, and polarization.

The story begins with the election of 2028, based on trends established much earlier. This is speculative science fiction of the near future. Could it soon become our present? I want to know what you think. Let me know at: dystopiandreamspress@outlook.com.

Other Books in the Sins of the Saviors Series

Prequel: The Network Apostate (2024)

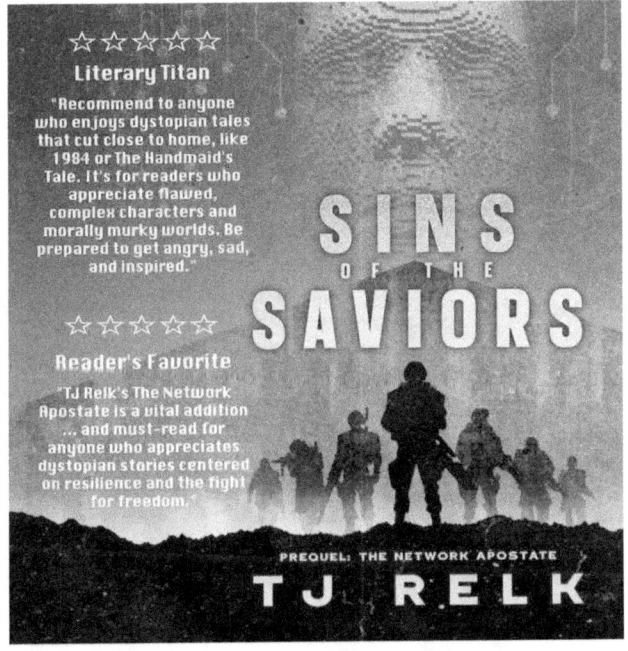

Book 2: The Price of Prosperity
(Coming in 2025)

Dystopian Dreams

dystopiandreamspress@outlook.com